The Adventures of the Lawndale Gang

by
Dan McMeans

"The Adventures of the Lawndale Gang," by Dan McMeans ISBN 978-1-63868-195-3 (hardcover).

Published 2025 by Virtualbookworm.com Publishing, P.O. Box 9949, College Station, TX 77842, US.

Contents

Introduction

The "Lawndale Gang" was a group of seven girls and nine guys who formed lasting bonds for many years. Most of us resided within Lawndale, Philadelphia, on various tree-lined streets.

We went through our coming-of-age years together starting at the age of 13. Our youthful years seemed to be ending when we went to our senior proms together. We had many fond memories as we went through our teenage years together. We laughed and cried as we experienced the growing pains that often come during the teenage years. But in the end, we survived these tumultuous years through shared experiences and relying on each other. These same values we passed on as we raised our own families.

These stories are about this group solving mysteries and going on numerous adventures. "The Coming of Age in Lawndale" is entirely true, but the others are fictional.

I love my friends for all the memorable events I experienced as a teenager. As I have gotten older, I like to think I am wiser now and believe that love is the universal fabric that connects us all, especially in the adventures with the Lawndale Gang.

The Coming of Age of Lawndale

Beginning at age thirteen, we would all meet at the corner of Magee and Oakley Streets to sit on the steps of a neighbor's house. We did this until we were 18 years old. Magee and Oakley will always hold a special place in our hearts because that's where we gathered each night. We did everything together, including many of us going to the proms at Northeast High School and Cardinal Dougherty High School in 1980.

Every Sunday, we played rough touch football with the older guys in the neighborhood. They would meet us at the top field of a park in Cheltenham, across from the railroad tracks. Our girlfriends would cross the tracks to the field to support our efforts. We brought blankets, munchies, and a radio to listen to the Eagles game. It was quite the event. The older guys were two or three years older than us; sometimes they won, and sometimes we won. Those were the days.

Another sport we regularly played was Playground Hockey, where ice hockey rules were followed, although we played on an asphalt surface. As our reputation grew, it caught the attention of a group of

1

guys from another neighborhood across the railroad tracks in Cheltenham, Pa. This rival neighborhood's hockey team was known as a fierce, formidable opponent. Confident in our ability, we agreed to play the game on their turf. However, when we arrived, we discovered their playing surface resembled a World Wrestling Federation wrestling cage. It was obvious that the team with the best physical prowess and fore-checking skills would win.

I knew this would be a brutal game as we walked up to their "hockey arena" with a 14-foot fenced enclosure. We were ready for battle with the girls behind us, and our minds were set on how to prevail. We were ready!

When we practiced any sport, we could transform the elements of city life around us into an arena of athletic discipline. Curbs would become out-of-bounds markers, telephone poles would become first-down markers, and trees and cars would become boundaries for goal lines and end zones. The elements of city life became the difference between winning and losing.

It was a tough battle between two determined hockey teams, but we relied not only on our skills, but also on our character and determination. As we played, an unspoken atmosphere settled in, challenging us to work as a team, believe in ourselves, and remember the sheer joy of winning.

As the seasons changed, so did our sports. The girls continued to be supportive but were starting to feel neglected. We weren't like other guys; we played sports all the time. The girls in our group were getting bored.

There was another group of guys meeting on a different corner down the street, whom we didn't care for. They weren't fortunate enough to have girls in their group. These guys started to entice the girls in our group to join them. Then, one day, the girls didn't show up at Magee and Oakley.

At first, we thought it was an aberration; then, we saw the girls hanging out with the other group of guys. We were beside ourselves, upset and hurt. We felt the girls had abandoned us, which made us feel even worse.

Several months passed, and we realized that the girls were an integral part of our group. They were very supportive of all our sporting events and social gatherings, and it bothered us that they were gone. Then, one day, the girls showed up at Magee and Oakley just as they had done many times before — like nothing happened. Everyone sat down and talked things out. We realized there were hurt feelings on both sides, but that none of us felt complete without the other.

One of the outspoken girls in the group expressed how they often felt overlooked. As we discussed it, the same girl said they realized we had something special in our group and wanted to return to continue the journey.

One memorable summer, we ran a 48-hour whiffle ball marathon for the Jerry Lewis Labor Day Muscular Dystrophy Telethon. My sister wrote an article about the upcoming whiffle ball marathon that appeared in the Northeast Philadelphia Times newspaper two weeks before the event. We got a permit to close down

Magee Street and set up schedules for the 48-hour tournament.

We made giant banners that we hung on Magee Street and Oakley Avenue. A neighborhood hardware store donated flood lamps so we could play throughout the night. We slept in reclining lawn chairs in the street and ate Fanti's pizza, which the owner donated for everyone to enjoy.

Even the neighbors on the block got involved. One of the girl's parents treated everyone to donuts one morning. The girls stood on the corner of Magee and Oakley St with buckets to collect donations from cars driving by while the guys played whiffle ball. This tournament turned into a community event. The group raised $1751 for the telethon and recognized the power of working together to achieve a goal.

Another project we undertook one summer was building a fort close to the railroad tracks on the Philadelphia side. With the money from our newspaper routes, we pooled enough to purchase wood and shingles to make a free-standing structure. We were proud of the elevated floor and roof that kept us dry in the rain. We met many nights a week, and our teenage conversations sometimes involved significant life topics. As Christmas neared, the girls prepared our spacious fort and decorated it for our annual Christmas gathering. The girls took pride in putting up the decorations that made our fort very festive over the holidays. At our Christmas gathering, much merriment was expressed for another joyful holiday. We expressed our gratitude for each other as another year ended.

We had an older boy in the neighborhood who was considered the "music maestro" in the neighborhood. He didn't hang out with us very often at our corner, but on numerous occasions, he would invite us to his rec room in his basement, where he had the most advanced stereo equipment around. With all his classic rock posters, he was the one who introduced us to music by bands like The Beatles, Led Zeppelin, The Who, Electric Light Orchestra, Aerosmith, Van Halen, and The Cars. He was the go-to guy for all the concert tickets when these acts came to town. We have fond memories of his devotion to music as a teenager.

Once we learned to drive, we ventured outside Lawndale. We all loved a trip to Greenwood Dairies in Langhorne, PA, where they served the area's largest portions of delicious homemade ice cream. This was part of our nostalgia growing up in Lawndale. We also spent a lot of time at Fanti's Pizza and a local Dairy Queen in Lawncrest. From time to time, when we were stopped at red lights, we would jump out and circle the cars, just acting silly, hoping to let everyone know that we were having a good time.

We all knew to meet at the corner of Magee and Oakley streets at the end of the day to collaborate and enjoy each other's company. This was our meeting place for quite some time, but it irritated a particular patrolman, Officer Fritz. He didn't like us "loitering" on the corner, even though we were a peaceful group that didn't bother anyone. Nevertheless, he was on a mission to disrupt us. For no reason, he would gather some of us up and charge us with a misdemeanor of disorderly conduct. The judge would then dismiss it, because it was meritless. We got tired of his antics, so we devised a plan to get back at him. About five of the guys had a secret meeting when snow was on the ground. We waited for his patrol car to pass our corner, and as it did, we unleashed a fury of snowballs. We heard the crackling noise of snowballs hitting the side of the patrol car as we ran away. We had the benefit of knowing all the paths and shortcuts around the houses on Magee Street. In our hearts, we knew there was no way he could catch us. We all met at our fort afterwards for high fives, celebrating how successful our revenge plan was executed.

Pennypack Park was our go-to destination for picnics, co-ed softball games, hiking, and campfires. These events led to many discussions and debates on general topics and life. Over several years, we went to Holiday Lakes in Bridgeboro (Delran), NJ. It was a big lake with a beach and an awesome ladder and dive platform in the center. We would have chicken fights with the girls on the guys' shoulders while in the lake. We had terrific times!

When we were about 16, we sometimes pitched tents in one of our backyards. The guys and the girls would have separate tents. Then, at 1 a.m., we would all get up to explore our surroundings on bikes and appreciate the serenity and peacefulness of the night. We observed milkmen delivering on their routes; a time-old practice of delivering bottles of milk to people's homes has become a memory of the past. We also saw bakeries delivering their rolls to delis in the area. This is the neighborhood businesses of the night. Then we sat on our bikes and watched the sun rise over the fields at Hasbrook and Magee with awe, watching the sky come to life to welcome a new day. Then, we returned to our tents to get some sleep.

On several occasions, we went to New Hope to see plays at the Bucks County Playhouse. After these performances, we would walk through New Hope, window shopping the quaint shops up and down Main Street.

One day, we decided to explore an abandoned mansion in Montgomery County called Strawberry Mansion. As we pulled up to the mansion, we wondered what life must have been like for this house in its heyday. The house was built at the end of the 1800s. It had a grand entrance with an impressive circular driveway and awe-inspiring front door. Walking through that door and seeing the majestic steps that led upstairs, we felt like we were returning to an earlier era.

We tried to imagine what life was like back then in this magnificent house. As we walked around, we couldn't help but notice the majestic steps leading upstairs. We cautiously walked through the house and found an elevator shaft that looked like it went down several flights. The cables were still intact and exposed. The guys were intrigued and wondered what could be on the lower levels, but the girls were not interested.

After some convincing from the guys, we all agreed to climb down one level using the exposed cables in the elevator shaft. Once we arrived at the basement level, it was pitch black! We couldn't see two feet ahead of us. As our eyes grew accustomed to the dark, we noticed a lot of debris around us. But there was something else.

We had an eerie feeling that something or someone was watching us. We kept hearing footsteps but couldn't see anything. Panic started to set in; we wanted to return to the elevator shaft, but how could we when we couldn't see? We slowly moved around as a group, searching for the light from the elevator shaft. The footsteps continued. It felt as if the footsteps were hostile, which gave us a sense of urgency to find the elevator shaft. Suddenly, we spotted the light and helped the girls up the elevator cables. Once all of us were on solid ground, we breathed a sigh of relief.

We wondered about that eerie feeling. Was it a malevolent ghost? Who knows...but we were grateful to return to the safety of our cars.

Prom season provided other memorable moments. Half of the group went to Northeast High School in Philadelphia, and the other half went to Cardinal Dougherty High School in Cheltenham. Fortunately, both proms were on different dates so everyone could go to each other's proms and have a great time. We had double the proms to look forward to! Clean and shiny cars would line Magee Avenue, and the procession of gals in prom gowns and the guys in their tuxedos would begin. Those were indeed the days.

The final prom in our senior year was the Cardinal Dougherty gala. We knew that the end of our teenage years was in sight, and a new era was upon us. The day after the Cardinal Dougherty High School Senior Prom, we all piled in our cars for one more trip to Wildwood, NJ.

As we sat on the beach mesmerized by the ocean and the rhythmic sound of the crashing waves, we felt the symbolism of the surf, which brought in the feeling that helped us realize changes were ahead. There would always be ups and downs, but at least the group knew we had built lasting memories from our teenage years together. We felt prepared for our future because we understood the supportive, caring, and nurturing relationships that come from a great group of friends. No matter what the future held for each of us, we knew we would always be available to support one another.

Lawndale Athletes against the Devil's Gate

The first part of this story is true, while the conclusion is pure fiction.

The Lawndale Gang met in our fort off Hasbrook and Magee Streets to discuss our next football opponent. We were surrounded by four large recreation centers where we played tackle football: Lawncrest, Fox Chase, Jardel, and Max Myers. Each recreation center could pull from a large pool of players when we played them. Our nucleus had eight guys from Magee and Oakley, and we filled in with other guys from nearby neighborhoods. We were a scruffy but talented team that believed we could win against all others, even though we had to play both offense and defense most of the time. We had our girls by our side who were always loyal and got us through many games. Back then, it was common for neighborhoods to compete with their own football equipment.

Our tenacious work ethic helped us through the three recreational centers, piling up victory after victory and setting us up for a showdown with Lawncrest Recreation Center. We knew we were going to be outmanned at 30 to our 11. Lawncrest was considered the cream of the crop. They had many more players to pull from and better equipment than we had, but we were known as a hard-hitting team with fortitude and grit in our bones. With our girls by our side, we were ready for battle. We knew as we met in the fort that we built with our own hands that this would be our ultimate test.

It was the day that we faced Lawncrest, and the football game was about to begin. The 11 of us knew we had to reach deep within ourselves in order to beat this team. As we prepared for kick-off, there was a spiritual presence among us; we knew this spiritual presence gave us the strength, confidence, and the courage to play our best with just 11 players, against a well-represented team with the best equipment.

As the game went on, and we were ahead in the score, we noticed they were bringing in older guys off the street, suiting them up, and putting them in the game. Throughout each quarter, our wounds piled up. But fortunately, we had our girls ready to bandage us up to keep us going so we could prevail against this opponent and win the game with conviction and fearlessness. Shortly after the game, six of the guys decided to cross the tracks to go into the top fields of Cheltenham Township, where they had a football field available for us to practice on as needed.

As we were practicing, a group member searched the woods for the football that had gotten away. As he looked for the football, he fell into a different dimension. The other group members got tired of waiting and went looking for him. We also fell into this alternate dimension when we found his prescription glasses on the ground. It wasn't long before the six of us were together in this place. This other dimension had a sinister feel to it, and it looked unnatural, as well. As we descended the path, a dark, transparent cloud suddenly appeared and kept us from walking. As we stood before this dark cloud, wondering what it was, we heard it speak to us. "I know you, but do you know who I am? Your triumphant ways of winning are no match for the Prince of Darkness — or should I say the Anti-Christ — but you may know me best as Satan."

A spokesperson from the group took a step towards the evil dark energy cloud and said, "I think I can speak for all of us and say that as long as God is with us, there is no power that can stand against us."

"You insolent bastards," said Satan. "Do you know how powerful I am?"

We responded: "Here's what we do know — you're going to have a front-row seat to us getting out of here."

Back at the fort, the girls noticed that we hadn't returned from practice and went to look for us at the field. The girls went to the top field and started looking for us, but all they found were our jackets and duffel bags.

As the girls sat together, worried and wondering where we might be, a bright light with wings appeared in front of them and said, "Do not be afraid, for I am Archangel Gabriel and I have come to inform you that your friends are in trouble and need your prayers. Your friends fell into an evil dimension and are battling Satan as we speak. You need to figure out how to re-open the gate to this other dimension to help your friends come home. This is your job. Before I leave you, I will show you where they were before they fell into the evil dimension. Good luck, and let's move forward with love and purpose, for God is always with you."

While the girls prayed, Satan's evil energy cloud started to break apart and go after the individual members of the team. To our alarm, this evil, insidious energy entered us and started to rise up our legs. It was a terrible feeling, and we got the impression that this evil energy was after our hearts to kill us. We decided for the time being we should disperse. As we traveled down the path ahead of us, Satan mocked us. "How dare you disrespect me. Now you will pay dearly and bow before me."

We continued down the path as the evil energy worked its way up our bodies. We came across a separation in the path, which was a very steep drop to certain death. The only way to cross it was to take a running start and leap over it. And that's what we did, collectively. As we all landed on the other side of the separated path, one of the guys fell short and was barely hanging on by a tree root from the side of the cliff. We rushed to his aid, helped him to his feet and sighed with relief when we were on the other side of the path.

Nevertheless, the evil energy clouds were still in us, trying to work their way up through our bodies so they could strangle our hearts.

"You can't run from what I sent into you, for I am an expert at human anatomy. What I sent into you will eventually choke your heart and extinguish your life," Satan said.

We continued down the path until we arrived at a cave. We cautiously entered the cave and explored our surroundings. We soon discovered a stone altar that must have been made by previous travelers who got trapped in this evil dimension.

On top of this stone altar was a horizontal slate with the Lord's Crucifix chiseled into the slate. We were very moved and inspired by this discovery, but we were still feeling the effect of the evil energy clouds as they moved deeper into our bodies. We looked for more clues and found an old leather scroll behind the altar. We unraveled the scroll and found information about the lost teachings of Zoroaster. He was a forward-thinking priest of his time and had great influence on Cyrus the Great, a Persian King who liberated the Jews from Babylonian captivity to resettle and rebuild in Jerusalem. This earned Cyrus an honored place in Judaism in 900 BCE. Meanwhile, the girls went home to do research on other dimensions and how to access them.

They knew the urgency of time was at hand. They found interesting information on the Internet regarding parallel universes that could exist in another dimension. They discovered the string theory, which suggests that subatomic particles are different notes on a tiny, vibrating string. This theory leaves the possibility of multi-dimensionality open. The harmonies of string theory correspond to the laws of physics, according to physicist Michio Kaku. With this information, the girls ran back to the top field and looked for the entry point to the evil dimension that Archangel Gabriel told them about. In this alternate universe, we continued to read these ancient scrolls, and were enlightened by the teachings of Zoroaster, a Persian priest. Zoroaster believed in contemplation, reflection, and meditation on God's work and personal spiritual growth.

We learned through these scrolls that the battle of good and evil is necessary, so man can achieve goodness through battling evil. We also learned that astrology, which is like a blueprint of a person's life, is a part of the philosophy of the priest Zoroaster, who was an influential preacher of his time. We had come to understand that maybe it was our destiny to battle Satan.

Together, we gathered at the stone altar and recited the Lord's Prayer. One of us remembered a quote from Jesus, that said, "If you have the faith as small as a mustard seed, you can say to this mountain – move and it will move from here to there. Nothing will be impossible to you!" This really inspired us. Then we made a prayer to our God for protection and strength, to propel us forward to do His will in His honor.

After our prayer, we stood up and one of us spoke for all of us and said to Satan, "Satan, you do not scare us with your bag of tricks, for there is one Divine True Power that is Omni and Supreme and it gives us eternal hope and strength to help us conquer all our obstacles." When the spokesperson finished, we felt a Divine Grace descend on us that helped us remove the evil dark energy clouds that were attempting to strangle our hearts.

We left the cave empowered with God's strength. Satan spoke to us as we left. "How dare you rise up against me"? We responded, "We're going to find a way home. Either you get out of our way, or you'll be run over."

The six of us continued back the same way we came. Meanwhile, the girls had set up a vigil at the gate that marked the entry to the dimension. They played music, hoping it would act as a beacon to guide us back home. As we navigated down the path, we could hear the music and realized the girls were trying to help us get home. Following the music, we found the gateway to the other dimension, which is our home, thanks to the girls.

As we walked through the dimension to home, the last person through turned around and said, "Satan, from the beginning of time, and throughout all the generations, there will always be One God, One Power and One Law Forever and Ever! For you have witnessed the power of God, where He is beyond all boundaries." Then all the boys were home and greeted by the girls and lots of group hugs and smiles ensued as the eleven of us gathered to celebrate our friendship.

The Lawndale Gang
and the Amazon

This story is both non-fiction and fiction because the group actually existed.

It came to our attention that one of our parents from the group had an illness that was unknown to the doctors, and the medical staff recommended that he look into alternative sources for a cure. One person in our group watched a television special on how some of the indigenous peoples in the Amazon River Basin used plant medicine to cure many of their illnesses. We decided to travel to Bolivia, where these tribes that use plant medicine live. These tribes live in the deepest parts of the rainforest, and travel by foot is needed to reach them.

We arrived in Bolivia and purchased a map to guide us to the Kallawaya Tribe. They are in the deepest parts of the rainforest and are known for their use of plant medicine, as well as their ancestral wisdom. We spent days on the trail as we advanced deeper and deeper into the rainforest. Being city kids, we weren't used to such dense foliage. Then, one day, as we were walking down the trail, we all fell into a large hole, and there was no way to climb the walls to escape. While in this hole, we started looking for another way to escape and found a trap door at the bottom. We opened the door, which provided a passageway out to a narrow ledge. We proceeded along the ledge, and to our surprise, we found several hieroglyphics on the walls.

Initially, we were mystified as to how hieroglyphics got on these walls. The artwork depicted what we thought were Egyptian men building a pyramid while looking up into the sky. This was a common theme throughout the several hieroglyphics we saw along the edge. We continued this perilous journey as rocks gave way beneath our feet.

As we continued down the narrow edge, we saw a clearing ahead, so we proceeded towards that area. As we got closer, we realized that the narrow edge led into a cave illuminated by a crack of sunlight on top. We looked around and to our surprise, we found an old wooden chest.

As we looked at the chest, we wondered what it could contain. And why was it in the cave? We opened the chest, and discovered information about the Tiwanuku Pyramid, built by the Tiwanuku tribe 5,000 years ago before the Inca dynasty. The information provided maps of how to get there and details about the structure itself. This included an explanation of how the math of the Tiwanaku pyramids, particularly in the structure known as *Akapana* is characterized by precise geometric calculations. This includes using right angles, alignments with cardinal directions, and evidence of the golden ratio, demonstrating a deep understanding of geometry and planning by the ancient Tiwanaku people.

This knowledge is seen in the precise fitting of massive stone blocks, creating complex patterns and symmetrical layouts across the site. Also, some of the stones were 65 tons. It remains a mystery how the ancient Tiwanaku tribe managed to quarry the necessary stones, known as andesite and transport them to the site. The andesite stone is an extrusive rock, forming when volcanic magma erupts, causing it to solidify. How they transported these 65-ton blocks 5,000 years ago to construct the pyramids intrigued us.

After reading this information, we were inspired to check out the Tiwanaku Pyramid for ourselves, after we found the Kallawaya tribe. As we exited the cave, we saw more hieroglyphics on the cave walls depicting the Tiwanaku tribe looking up at the sky as they were building the geometric structures.

As we left the cave, we found a winding path descending the hill through a thick, lush forest with brush on both sides. We could see the village below with their lanterns on top of bamboo sticks from the hill where we stood. As we continued down towards the village, we were met by one of the Kallawaya tribe chiefs, and he invited us into their celebration honoring the nature spirits. After the celebration, we sat with the tribe's medicine men and explained our situation to him. We explained the illness of one of our member's fathers. The medicine man went into his hut and came out with a plant medicine remedy that he said would help. We were very grateful to the

Kallawaya Tribe for their kindness and willingness to help.

We looked at our maps and decided to explore the Tiwanaku pyramids, specifically the one known as *Akapana*

As we walked down the path towards the Tiwanaku Pyramids, we came across a large divide in the path with a plunge to certain death. We were baffled about how to cross this section to continue our journey. However, we saw a sturdy vine available that we thought we could use to cross the gorge separating us and the pyramids. We tugged on the vine, which seemed sturdy, and decided to cross the valley, hoping that the vine would not give way as we crossed the canyon. We proceeded to cross, but the vine became looser with each crossing. As the final girl crossed, the vine gave way. We were in a panic as she fell.

Fortunately, she descended onto a canyon incline, where she tumbled as she tried to slow down her descent. She finally reached out and grabbed a loose tree root that was upended on the canyon incline, stopping her tumbling and stabilizing her. We watched in terror as she finally came to a halt. We told her we were on our way to help and bring her back to safety.

We made our way down into the canyon until we found her 20 feet from the edge of the cliff, and we made a human chain that would connect each of us as we descended the incline. Once we reached her, we were all relieved and collectively supported each other as we continued down the trail toward the pyramids.

As we approached the outskirts of the pyramids, we found a hollow cavity in the ground that intrigued us, so we checked it out. Once inside, it appeared to be a passageway, so we followed the path, wondering where it might lead us. Then we started to see more hieroglyphics on the walls, and this told us we were getting close to the pyramids.

We continued down the path until we found markings on an entranceway that looked regal, so we investigated and found several caskets. We were amazed and looked at the caskets with wonder, as one particular casket looked especially regal. Since we were on a quest for knowledge, we decided to move the casket cover of the tomb. We collectively moved the stone cover, which revealed an old king from the past. What was intriguing was that there were clay tablets buried with him.

The clay tablets read, "We are the Tiwanaku tribe; please respect the structures that we built to honor the nature spirits. These structures should be remembered for their location and the sacrifices that went into creating them. We had aid and assistance that lifted our spirits during construction."

We thought about what this could mean. We thought back to the information in the chest and remembered the advanced geometry and the fittings of the massive stones, which were 65 tons. We resealed the king's tomb and proceeded to work on this mystery. We tried to connect all the pieces. Advanced geometry 5,000 years ago, massive 65-ton stones precisely fitted into the pyramid, then we started to think about the mysteries of the Egyptian pyramids and Stonehenge. All were built with advanced calculus and physics.

And then there were the hieroglyphics with the people of the tribe looking up at the sky. Could the Tiwanaku tribe have been visited by an advanced race to assist them?

We continued to explore the cavern as we learned more about the truth of the origins of the Tiwanaku tribe. We came across a rock that seemed to be out of place compared to the other rocks. When we removed the rock from the wall, we found another clay tablet with the words, "We came in peace from far away to assist mankind on Earth with structures to inspire them. We use precision in our building in the hope mankind on Earth will someday better understand us."

This message from the advanced race rattled us and really made us think of the circumstances of today with all the sightings of UFOs lately. We were starting to think that we were being visited for a higher purpose. Could these UFOs be from the same race that helped our early human ancestors?

As we exited the pyramids, we felt a sense of hope that our early ancestors were visited with a message of constructive wisdom. While the human race moves forward, it's comforting to know that we are all one in the pursuit of knowledge.

The Lawndale Gang and the Law of Attraction

The benefits of Law of Attraction are real as are the people in the story. The elements of the story, however, are fiction.

As humans, we go through different levels of consciousness. Right now, we are at the tail end of the Pisces level of awareness which limits us from our senses and embodiments. We are at the beginning of the Aquarius level of awareness which means we have more opportunities to be connected to our inner being. We are asked to be more conscious of our behavior than ever before.

One day I retreated to one of my favorite reading areas beside a creek in Chalfont, Pennsylvania. There is a large horizontal root that extends from the tree, which provides the perfect place to read one of my spiritual books. On this particular day, I rose and looked up at this impressive old tree and saw the light from the sun filtering through the branches and hitting a hole in the trunk of the tree in a way that lifted my spirits. I went to take a closer look and stuck my hand into the hole where I felt a glass bottle and pulled it out.

To my surprise, it appeared to be an old wine bottle with a piece of paper inside it. I pulled out the paper and it was a map with some instructions. The language looked old but it was legible. The writing referred to the importance of humanity moving forward in accordance with the Aquarius levels of consciousness. The map said the secrets of the Laws of Attraction were beneath the metallic crucifix at Saint Mary Basilica Church in Poland.

I took the map and went home and showed it to my other Lawndale friends and we shared it with one of their fathers. The man was a linguistics professor who could understand the ancient Italian writings that, to our surprise, were from the time of Galileo. Galileo was an astronomer who challenged the doctrine at the that time that the Earth was the center of the universe, and the sun rotated around the Earth rather than the Earth rotating around the sun.

The map also included notes on how to pass down ancient universal laws to assist the human race in getting to the next level of spiritual consciousness , to open up the human spirit to reach the Aquarius level of the mind. These laws were called the Laws of Attraction and were also passed on by our forefathers of knowledge; individuals like Plato, William Shakespeare, George Washington, Ludwig Von Beethoven, and Ralph Waldo Emerson.

George Washington concealed the Laws of Attraction, so they wouldn't fall into the hands of the enemy. From what we know, the Laws of Attraction are about sustaining positive thoughts that could bring things into materialization. With this in mind, we can bring ideas into materialization. For instance, your mental attitude directly affects your life's outcome. The power of manifestation is realized when we combine positive thoughts with taking steps toward our goals. By combining visualization ideas with a strong work ethic and courage, we can achieve our objectives with greater efficiency.

This really intrigued us, so we collectively decided to take an anthropology class at an affiliate campus of Temple College, which was not far from where we lived. The curriculum required us to explore the depths of the human spirit as it relates to applying positive thinking in relation to manifestation. We were divided into groups and each of us was allowed to pursue our projects separately. We decided to pursue the journey of manifestation that was passed down by others who were knowledgeable.

Collectively, we had to figure out how to get to Saint Mary Basilica Church in Poland, where the secrets of how to manifest materialization could be found. The map said the secrets of the Laws of Attraction were beneath the metallic crucifix on the wooden table.

We heard about a travel agency that offered a sailboat that crossed the Atlantic and we thought this would be an exciting way to cross the high seas. This sailboat was a replica of the sailboats of the 16th century, which was very intriguing. It had a sundial on it, which helped the captains of the past navigate through the high seas.

Shortly after we arrived in Poland, we entered the church and approached the altar. We prayed the Lord's Prayer before we approached the golden crucifix. We lifted it and found a pouch beneath it. We took the pouch to a safe place in the church and opened it, and found that it referred to some of the benefits of manifestation, which occur on the universal consciousness level that unites all things.

One of the Founding Fathers, Richard B. Moore, was a of the signer of the Constitution. He left secrets when he was a diplomat visiting Poland, and the map led us to a book that was in the Saxon State Library that existed during colonial times. The book we had to find in the library was called *Ancient Secrets Revealed* as it would provide further knowledge on the secrets of manifestation to help mankind.

We were up early the next morning in Poland. Due to the nature of our cause to bring humanity to new heights of spirituality by bringing material things into fruition, we discovered it also attracted dark evil forces that opposed us in our attempts. We were not aware of the depth and desperation that the forces of evil were willing to take in order to stop us.

We stood hand-in-hand because our group was committed to our cause as we stood tall against the Prince of Darkness who spoke to us, "I know what you're here for, and I will stop you with all my evilness. For I will demonstrate the true power of my darkness to you. I will never let you fully educate anyone on the powers of manifestation."

Our group responded, "As we stand together, we oppose you, as we are strong in our faith. Since faith is stronger than evil, and we are one in cause and purpose."

Satan replied, "I will crush you and make you bow down before me."

Our group said in unison, "You underestimate the strength of our collective will for God is our rock and our salvation."

The Saxon State Library was located in Dresden, Poland, and was built in 1556. As we travelled, our driver felt a force that tried to take over the wheel, and he had to fight this force, which he determined was evil.

A huge battle ensued for control over the wheel of the vehicle as the driver was trying to avoid other cars on the road and trees along the roadside. This battle raged on between good and evil until the driver started to recite the 23rd Psalm, which emphasizes "I will fear no evil."

Finally, we arrived at the Saxon State Library. Once there, we looked for the book, *Ancient Secrets Revealed* and we checked in with the Library Assistant. She said that she had no idea what we were talking about. However, we got the impression from the look on her face that there was more to the situation. We agreed to oblige her and moved on and looked around.

We looked for anything that seemed peculiar or out of place. We had a suspicious feeling that maybe the book was in an area that wasn't disclosed to the public, so we kept looking.

We eventually found a picture frame and when we looked behind it, we found a lever. The library was almost empty, so we pulled the lever and a library wall opened to reveal a secret room with an ancient desk containing an inscription on the side by Richard B. Moore, who was a diplomat and a signer of the Constitution. There was a bookshelf where we found the book *Ancient Secrets Revealed*, with the signatures of William Shakespeare, George Washington, Ludwig Von Beethoven, Ralph Waldo Emerson, and Galileo Galilei.

As we studied its meaning, we heard a voice speaking to us, and we soon realized its evil origin as it said, "If you leave this library, I will crush you and make you bow down before me, because I will never let you teach humanity and the principles of manifestation."

One of the girls took a step closer to where she thought the voice was coming from and said, "We believe we're on a mission from God to enlighten humanity with the principles of manifestation; we believe that Faith is stronger than evil and fear. And that good must triumph over evil, that we must go forward with the strength of God to prevail against all obstacles." So, we gathered up our things to exit the library with renewed spiritual strength to propel us forward against all odds.

We thought the best place to read the ancient material would be in a park at a picnic table where we could pray to God for protection, knowing that the nature spirits are strong and would help diminish any demonic voices from being heard. With the understanding of the existing benefits of the art of manifestation from our earlier research, we started to unravel the sources and expectations in depth.

The book said that we limit ourselves and our abilities when we give into limited beliefs, fear, pessimism and doubt. It went on to say that if you look at yourself with these perceptions, then you are limiting your abundance and prosperity when it comes to rewarding yourself with the principles of the universe.

As we read these ancient words, we were inspired to learn that it all starts with love being at the base of all functionalities. From that point, we begin to prepare the mind to bridge the gap between positive thinking and fear, and allowing ourselves to free the mind. Boundless possibilities can occur when the brain can take in positive messaging and absorb it in the prefrontal cortex, which will transmit out from the subcortical parts of the brain. The messages will then go out to the universe, which knows all your needs and helps bring things to fruition.

Once we read the ancient material, we felt an obligation to spread the news throughout America by going to an agent and having him start booking dates for us at college campuses throughout the nation. Before we journeyed home, we stood by the lake hand-in-hand in solidarity and prayed to God, asking him for his protection: "Protect us in trouble wherever we go and keep evil far from us as we do Your calling. No matter where we are, we will look up to you as our Protector, the One who fights for us every day. "

We found a touring agent who has secured many dates for us to speak about the benefits of manifestation. We are excited to help spread the word about helping people bring to fruition the benefits of manifestation, and we feel so blessed that this responsibility has been given to us. We hope we made our ancestors of knowledge proud.

Let's move forward with love and purpose, realizing that everybody has an opportunity to fulfill their purpose and build momentum for a bigger and brighter outcome. We can bring our future into reality. Let's take all that life has to give. We can do this. We can move mountains together!

The Lawndale Gang and the Altar of Spartacus

This story is both part non-fiction and fiction with storytelling because the group existed.

The father of one of the Lawndale members worked at the Smithsonian Institute. He passed along word to the Lawndale Gang that the Institute was providing an award to any person or group who finds the legendary Spartacus Altar, which has been passed down through many generations. Spartacus was a Roman soldier before his enslavement, then turned gladiator and performed in the Roman Colosseum to win and entertain the crowds of the Roman Republic. The award was significant enough that it motivated us to look into and find Spartacus's Altar. We quickly packed and flew to Europe, and then boarded a train bound for Rome.

While on the train, we heard about a high-stakes poker game that was taking place that night. One of the guys in our group was a strong poker player, so we arranged for him to be at the poker game.

31

When we arrived, there were six guys seated at the table. The poker game continued until there were only two players left. We could tell the guy across the table was a seasoned poker player, and he had his loyal friends with him as well. We watched the currency pile up on the table as both players looked at their cards. The Lawndale poker player put down his cards and said, "I Call." The other poker player said, "I'm out of money, but I can offer you a historical treasure map of incredible importance, and I would like to offer it up as collateral to match your offer."

We accepted his offer, and our guy won the hand. We took our loot back to our room, but before we left, the man who lost the treasure map said, "Let's hope you can handle what you may find in that treasure map." We were a little baffled as to what he said, but nevertheless, we continued to our room.

We retreated to the girls' room, counted the money and unraveled the treasure map. To our shock and dismay, the treasure map led to a chamber in the Vatican Museum in Rome, where the Lost Gospel of Thomas is located. According to the treasure map, the lost teachings of Jesus, which did not make it into the Bible could also be found there. We were astonished that this historical data fell into our laps. As we climbed into our beds for a good night's rest, little did we know that loyal followers to the poker player who lost the treasure map were planning to break in to the girls' room to steal back the treasure map.

Once the intruders were inside the girls' room, looking for the treasure map, one of the girls woke up due to the noise. She woke another girl, and whispered to her that there was someone in the room. At this point, they were frightened, as they watched mini-flashlights dance around in their room Now, all the girls from Lawndale have taken several martial arts classes to help them in emergency situations like this. As one Lawndale girl approached an intruder, he quickly grabbed her from behind and tried to control her body movement by grabbing her hair forcefully.

The Lawndale girl grabbed both of his hands from behind and locked them in place, moving beside him and forcing his arms behind his back. The Lawndale girl then flipped him and put her foot on his throat, while yelling to the Lawndale guys for help. The other girl fought the other intruder using a high kick side winder, knocking him out. With both intruders incapacitated, the guys came rushing to the girls' aid. But before they arrived, the intruders awoke, broke free and escaped. The guys arrived to comfort the girls, hid the treasure map, and started planning their next move once they arrived in Rome.

We arrived in Rome and started to follow the treasure map, which led us into the underworld beneath Rome. It was an eerie sewer system riddled with rats. As we followed the treasure map underneath the city, we searched for clues until we discovered a crucifix mounted right beyond the ladder walls that led upward. Per the treasure map, this should lead us to a chamber in the Vatican Museum. We climbed the ladder and removed a large ceramic tile from the floor, and arrived in the chamber where the Gospel of Thomas was stored.

We looked around for markings on where we could find this ancient manuscript. Suddenly, one of the guys recognized a symbol from when he studied mysticism in college. He realized that this symbol belonged to Archangel Sandalphon, who is known for his teachings that help people to understand the soul's lessons.

"This must be it," we said collectively and opened the drawer and found the Gospel of Thomas, which was never included in the Bible. Recognizing this was important and should be shared with the world, we took it with us. We exited the chamber with the scroll in hand, planning to deliver it to the Smithsonian Institute.

We felt the best place to read the scroll was at a public park with picnic tables, so we could spread the scroll out. Once we arrived, we unraveled the scroll and read some of the lost teachings of Jesus Christ, according to the Gospel of Thomas. Some of the passages are as follows:

"If the Father's imperial rule is in the sky, then the birds of the sky will precede you. If the Father's rule is in the sea, then the fish will precede you. Rather, the Father's imperial rule is inside of you and outside of you. When you know yourselves, then you will be known and you will understand that you are the children of the Living Father. But if you do not know yourselves, then you will live in poverty."

"The only thing that really exists is your divine spirit or your Divine Soul, which is identical in its quality to God himself."

"Those who seek should not stop seeking until they find."

In its entirety, there are over 100 sayings in the Gospel of Thomas. The picnic table where they spread out the ancient scroll was off the beaten path and, as we were going back to the hotel, saw another picnic table that held an ancient, opened Bible. We were perplexed because we didn't see it on the way as we walked by the first time.

We were really mystified as to how the Bible ended up here. There wasn't anyone in sight. Nevertheless, there was a Bible on the table that wasn't there before. We agreed to look at the page to see if we could get any meaning from it. Interestingly, we were inspired and moved by the Psalm on the page, which was Psalm 133, verse 1.

"Behold, how good and how pleasant it is for the brethren to dwell together in Unity."

We pondered what this meant. Was this Psalm referring to us? And what about this Bible that seemed to appear out of nowhere? Suddenly, we saw a car coming up the road, and knew it was the follower loyal to the poker player who lost the treasure map.

As we gathered our things, we saw a beautiful buck deer walk into the open and gaze at us with a long stare. It was as if the deer was trying to tell us something, but it then went back into the brush. Soon after that, a thick fog rolled in off the lake and started to create a wall between us and the car coming up the road. Was the buck trying to tell us something? Did the nature spirits come to our aid as we safely left the park?

We woke up the next morning in pursuit of the Spartacus Altar, which took us to the Roman Colosseum. We tipped the tour guide generously, so we could spend an hour in the Spartacus' cell. It is believed that Spartacus prayed to God at his altar in his cell before he entered the Colosseum. We looked around his cell and found a quote by the prophet Isaiah on a boulder in the back of the cell.

"Thou will keep him in perfect peace whose mind is stayed on thee." We took a closer look at edges of the boulder and we could see a crease outlining the boulder. We thought the Altar may be behind the boulder. We and carefully removed the boulder and discovered a space between the two walls. In this space, we found the Spartacus Altar, which held three candles and a religious necklace, which was made up of three stones to reflect the Holy Trinity.

It is said that he took off his necklace and placed it on the Altar with his three candles to pray to God. We had brought bags with us in case we found the altar. So, we put the boulder back and placed the altar in the bag, but needed a diversion in order to get past the guards.

After a long discussion, two of the Lawndale girls grudgingly volunteered to flirt with the two guardsmen as we snuck by with the Spartacus Altar remnants in a bag. We realized that the total finality of our goal is what mattered the most.

It's been a long journey that helped us reveal the Gospel of Thomas. We hoped this would bring to light many of Jesus' sayings that were previously unknown. It was also our honor to bring to the Smithsonian Institute the Spartacus Altar, which encouraged us from the beginning that good intentions naturally build up momentum to higher causes. Then we all went back to our rooms to reflect on our mission, which felt like a blessing from God.

Our group is now much older, but we like to reminisce about our coming-of-age togetherness, which bonded our friendship with one another in love and purpose.

Christmas is in Jeopardy

This story is both part non-Fiction and fiction with storytelling because the group existed.

We decided as a group to go to the Christmas Village in Center City, Philadelphia, an outdoor market where vendors sell a variety of Christmas items. As we walked around, we came upon an old wise man selling ancient books from the past, and we started to ask him about the true meaning of Christmas.

He told us that he hears whispers from the North Pole, and there might not be Christmas this year due to problems. The wise book seller heard that an Anti-Christ gang chained up Santa's reindeer so they couldn't fly, and he is hoping someone comes to their rescue.

The Lawndale Gang understood the situation's urgency and gathered for the long trip to the North Pole. This took some planning and figuring out how to get to our destination in the North Pole where Santa Claus' village is located. We found out we could go to 30th Street Station and take a train. It would take us several days to reach the village where Santa's Workshop is located.

While at the bar on the train, one of the passengers took an interest in one of the girls. In fact, he was increasingly making advances that made her feel uncomfortable. The boys took offense to his overtures, and we stood between our girl and the unruly man. A staring contest ensued, and his nearby buddies backed him up. Then the man in question pulled a knife on the Lawndale boys, thinking they would back down from such a threat. But the Lawndale boys were schooled in the knowledge that faith is stronger than fear. Faith includes discipline, patience, focus, and not overreacting – virtues that are stronger than fear.

As the boys stood their ground, the man with the knife backed up and whispered to his buddies, "What kind of power is this?" As he put the knife away and continued to retreat, he did some soul-searching as to what this meant. This is how our universe works when faith is confronted with fear.

We went as far as possible by train, and had to travel on foot for the rest of the journey to the North Pole. The Lawndale Group used snowshoes that looked like tennis rackets to help walk in the snow as they pursued their quest. Night fell as we were walking, so we pitched tents. But it wasn't long before we were attacked by vicious wolves who cornered us. We tried to fend off the wolves, but they were relentless.

Suddenly, six owls with their five-foot wing spans came down on the wolves, dive-bombing them until they relented and dispersed. From what we know of this area, it must have been the Snowy Owls, which are native to this area. It is known that they are mysterious, but we are thankful for their intervention.

As we continued, we looked up to the sky and spotted a Snowy Owl. It appeared to be guiding us. As the day went on, we were getting tired, so we set up for camp and built a fire. But it wasn't long before the Evil Witch of the North Pole appeared and warned us. "I'm the one who inspired the Anti-Christ group that chained up Santa's Reindeer. Now, I am warning you to not get involved with this."

One of the Lawndale girls retorted, "Love is the ultimate power in the universe and that is the purpose of our cause." Suddenly, a nearby tree started to come to life with movement in its limbs and trunk. It uprooted itself from the dirt as it walked towards us. It was terrifying to watch. Then suddenly, the tree's long branches grabbed one of the girls and tried to put her in its menacing trunk mouth. It didn't work, since the boys were trying to dislodge the girl from the tree's clutches. Then suddenly, one of the boys grabbed a log from the fire pit, and another boy joined him. They approached the tree waving their fire logs, which caught one of the tree's limbs on fire. The tree dropped the girl and retreated to its natural position.

We continued to follow the owl for direction, and we came upon a house along our path. We were cold, and the woman inside invited us in to get warm and have some hot chocolate. As we sat around the table, one of her daughters, who was six years old, said they heard whispers from Santa's workshop that there might not be a Christmas this year.

"Is that true," she asked. Our hearts sank, not wanting to disappoint the child. So, the Lawndale girls, with their nurturing spirits, told the young girl that we were doing everything in our capacity to ensure that there was a Christmas this year. Before we left thanked the woman and the family for their hospitality, and continued our journey.

We climbed the mountain, and once we reached the top, we could see Santa's Workshop. We decided to pitch our tents on top of the mountain. We started a campfire, then a swirling particle of energy appeared, which resembled a vortex. It materialized as a spirit and said, "I am Goddess Sedna, Goddess of the North Pole. The Anti-Christ group empowered by the Evil Witch did psychological damage to Santa's reindeer. Please take this pixie dust blessed by me to help the reindeer fly." We opened up one of the bags we weren't using and Goddess Sedna blessed it with pixie dust. "God always has faith in His people, and you have an important mission to accomplish. Good Luck and Godspeed!"

We descended the mountain and met with Santa. He told us all his concerns about the Anti-Christ motives of depriving children of their toys and requested our help. We explained to Santa that we met with Goddess Sedna, and she gave us the blessed pixie dust to help the reindeer fly. While we were there, we asked Santa for the true story of Santa Claus. He explained, "Saint Nicholas was a fourth-century bishop known for his generosity and gift-giving.

This caught on with Dutch immigrants who celebrated Saint Nicholas by leaving their shoes out for Christmas. They were then given a treat in their shoes.

And the spirit was given to him to fulfill the hearts of children worldwide."

After Santa explained the origin of Santa Claus, we confronted the Anti-Christ Gang, using baseball bats we found in his workshop. They quickly backed down and ran off. Then we unshackled the reindeer, and Santa was ready to spread joy and happiness to children around the world. He unleashed the reindeer, and they started to gallop. But they were so distraught from being chained up, they were reluctant to fly.

Santa was extremely worried because he could see a cliff in the distance and the reindeer were reluctant to fly as Santa and the sleigh approached the cliff's edge. So, he spread the blessed pixie dust all over the reindeer. As they took their perilous leap, the reindeer suddenly realized they were on a journey to fulfill the dreams of children, and the sleigh rose into the sky.

With excitement and enthusiasm, Santa called, "Now Dasher, now Dancer, now Prancer and Vixen! On Comet, we have a mission to fulfill and lift the spirits of mankind".

Dracula's Castle

This story is both fiction and nonfiction, with storytelling about our group that helped other people solve mysteries and problems, which put us on many adventures.

We decided to go on vacation to Romania, where we thought it would be exciting to stay in the legendary Dracula's Castle, also known as Bran's Castle, in Transylvania. The lure was that you could stay in an actual castle bedroom and attend castle festivities throughout the week. Each of us had our own bedroom.

The castle was built in 1377, and we were getting ready for the night's festivities, which included a dinner feast with entertainment, similar to the way the castle operated long ago. We were required to dress in period clothing. which the castle provided. We danced and had fun, relaxed and enjoyed each other's company.

The next morning, we noticed that each one of our bedframe posts had markings on them that looked like some kind of language. One of our members took a picture and sent it to her father who is a linguistics professor. At first her father was not familiar with this language. After doing some research, he discovered that it was the Akkadian language, an ancient Semitic language, spoken by the Babylonians during the Babylonian Empire, around 1900 BCE.

We were very confused as to why these ancient markings were on the bedframes. The girl's linguistics professor father interpreted the marking on the bedframes, which read, "We are the Babylonians, and we are proud of our engineering for our water transportation for our hanging gardens. These engineering secrets are in the seamstress room." We Googled this phrase on our phones as to what this could be, and discovered that the Babylonians constructed a very advanced aqueduct system that carried water from the Euphrates River to their Hanging Gardens of Babylon, which is one of the Seven Wonders of the World

The true genius of their engineering is how far they built the underground watercourse. It was approximately 40 miles long, amazing for that time and era. After learning so much about the Hanging Gardens of Babylon, we were anxious to retrieve the engineering secrets that had been passed down by ancestors of the Babylonians who put the marking on the bedframes.

We thought the Smithsonian Institute would want to have this information. We asked a member of the housekeeping staff where the seamstress room in the castle, and she pointed down the hallway. We arrived at the seamstress room and started to look around for clues but couldn't find any. There was, however, an old wooden sewing box that looked very timeworn.

We looked in there and didn't see anything, initially. After a closer look, however, we discovered a hidden compartment in the sewing box. We opened it and there was a leather scroll that had the secrets of how the irrigation system by the Babylonians was constructed 4,000 years ago. We put it in our bag to take it home safely.

We woke up the next day and realized that while all the rest of our rooms were exactly the same, one room had an old metal container on the mantle above the fireplace. We agreed as a group to look inside the container, and we were shocked to realize that it was Dracula's diary. We took the diary over to the nearest table to look at it. It was like looking back in history to the mid-1600s. The assistant to Dracula wrote a diary entry after Dracula passed away. He mentioned that he was closing in on how to kill him because he knew the harm he was doing to women. The assistant figured out that Dracula was poisoned and he documented his slow death in the diary and didn't have long to live. Separate from that, Dracula's family was very suspicious on how he died and sought redemption.

One day, as we were heading to our rooms for the night, one of the Lawndale Boys said "Wait a minute. something is not right here." He was referring to a print of the castle and the grounds with the graveyard close by. "This particular grave had fresh dirt on it where each time I passed it and for the last few days, the dirt was settled." We all took a closer look at the grave. Dracula's family throughout generations had suspected wrongdoing, so they left several clues behind hoping that someone would investigate Dracula's passing, so he could rest in peace.

We took a closer look at the gravestone and noticed that at the bottom right-hand side, there was the symbol of the Masonic Lodge. We know this because one of our fathers was a Freemason, and he was proud to show the symbol. Normally, there is an oval and a 90-degree angle, which reflects integrity and respect, but this symbol was upside down, meaning that there was something wrong. We felt that Dracula's family was leaving us clues and wanted someone to bring justice to this situation. We finished the day and went back to our rooms.

Once settled in bed, the bedframe headboards opened up, captured us, and put us on a rail going backwards. Our gang was united in the underworld under the castle. We walked around the mysterious area and eventually discovered a large lake with row boats. We were trying to take all this in and pondered the meaning of it all. We found row boats on a dock next to a lake. The row boats must lead us somewhere, we thought. We got in the row boats and paddled for a while until we came across a deserted shack. We looked around and discovered it was the assistant's shack.

We came to the conclusion that he privately served as a member of the Masonic Lodge and believed in its principles of brotherhood and truth as a part of their fraternity. We found an old pair of trousers and, as we took a closer look at the belt of the trousers, we found a hidden zipper in the interior of the belt. We looked inside and found a note. "Floorboard marked in the center of shack with slight proliferation on board." So, we investigated what this meant, found the floorboard in question, pulled it up, and found a bag. We opened the bag to find a stake with a note from the assistant. "If Dracula dies of natural causes, he will have the ability to come back like a ghost, haunt women while they sleep and drain them of their vitality for his own sustenance. For the love of God, please take this stake and, if you see Dracula's ghostly form, drive this stake into his heart. For this stake possesses natural wood, which would propel against the unnatural."

So, we took the stake, as we recognized the huge responsibility had been given to us. From Dracula's diary, we determined that he did die of natural causes. We were worried for our girls because the myth is that he comes at night to drain women of their vitality for his own desires We told the girls to have their cell phones by their side while they slept, and if they saw something odd to call us.

Around 2 a.m., one of the girls woke up in a panic and had the feeling that someone was near her. She called the boys, but before she knew it, she saw the ghost of Dracula trying to drain her essence. She put up a mirror that was close to her bed to deflect the extracting energy and screamed as the Lawndale boys came running into her room. We saw what was happening and quickly, surrounded the ghost of Dracula . We could see that he was trying to get away and knew we had to finish the job. We then saw a room deodorant spray bottle that contained aloe and other natural ingredients, and we knew this would be handy in our greatest hour of need. So, one of the guys grabbed the spray bottle and said, "Let Archangel Michael seal the door where evil dwells so we may prevail." Then he started to spray the ghost of Dracula. As he sprayed, Dracula's power started to diminish, we grabbed the stake and thrusted it through his heart with purpose, for we knew that good must prevail over evil.

The Lawndale Gang enjoyed the rest of the week participating in all the festivities for there is always tomorrow to start the day anew with putting one step in front of the other to move forward with love and purpose.

Mr. Montgomery's Walk through Lawndale

My name is Mr. Montgomery. I've walked a lot in the Northeast section of Philadelphia over the last 30 years. A local newspaper asked me to recall my favorite neighborhood to walk through in this part of the city

There isn't much I haven't seen during my last thirty years, but I do recall walking through a neighborhood with its own sound. I can't remember that small community, but it had a mystique different from all the other neighborhoods.

As I walked through this area, I heard voices crackling with urgency. I heard hockey sticks constantly banging against the street, hungry for the puck. If it wasn't hockey, it was a wiffleball clanging off the back of a garage where the strikes zone was located.

When I approached the Lawndale neighborhood, I would listen from a distance to what sounded like a rough touch football game, but the sounds of the game were different. I heard metallic sounds from this game and as I moved in to get a closer look, I discovered the

49

intensity of a rough, touch football game that resulted in the hard jolts of bodies slamming against vehicles.

This Lawndale group was known for their togetherness and athletic prowess, but I hoped to catch their attention for a different reason. Captivated by their remarkable talent for unraveling mysteries, I reached out to them to explore a deep-seated family enigma, and they eagerly agreed to hear my story.

***

We remember that day when Mr. Montgomery approached us to discuss his family's history. He told us about his aunt who lost her life 375 years ago in Salem, Massachusetts. She was a gifted psychic, but was accused of witchcraft by the townsfolk. Before they could put her on trial, she chose to commit suicide, knowing that anyone tried for witchcraft would ultimately be hanged.

However, it was passed down in his family that she died with secrets about past events that Mr. Montgomery hoped to unravel. During psychic readings and deep meditations, his aunt picked up visions regarding a lost pirate treasure off Hawaii's Big Island. Captain Thomas Cavendish, a 16th century pirate, is said to have buried $5 million in gold and silver. Over the years, the family continued to pass down the story of these psychic visions and now Mr. Montgomery sought help from the Lawndale Gang to locate the treasure.

"She is said to be buried with a pendant necklace around her neck," said Mr. Montgomery "This pendant has vital location details as to where the treasure can be found. Her body is in a family crypt in Salem, Massachusetts."

We talked amongst ourselves and then told Mr. Montgomery we'd take this assignment if we could have half the treasure. This money would help us with our college education.

We arrived in Salem and entered Mr. Montgomery's family crypt, which was full of snakes and rats. With sticks we located nearby to push away the snakes and rats, we entered the crypt and located his aunt's coffin. As we carried it outside, the girls put their hands over their faces, and the guys braced themselves for what was inside.

Although the body was very decayed, the necklace was visible! The chain holding the pendant was broken but the actual pendant, which contained a large sapphire, was still intact. Behind the sapphire, a small clasp revealed a piece of paper and a small compass. We removed the paper and discovered it contained vital nautical charts on where to locate Captain Cavendish's treasure.

We flew from Philadelphia to Monterey Regional Airport in Salinas, California. From there, we decided to experience the high seas like the pirates. We took a tall ship with nautical equipment from the 16th century as we set sail for Big Island of Hawaii.

We arrived at the reef of the Big Island. Because our sailing ship was so large, we had to take two inflated rafts to go onto shore, but while we were paddling, a huge wave crashed into us and overturned our rafts.

As we were trying to gather our rafts from beyond the surf, the boys saw the fin of what looked like a great white shark bearing down on the girls. The boys immediately intervened and put themselves between the girls and the shark. As the shark approached the boys, they remembered what they had seen on television programs about shark attacks. They knew their only hope was to try to gouge the eyes of the shark or cut its underbelly, where it is most vulnerable.

Within seconds, the shark was upon them, circling and whipping his tail with great force. One of the boys dove below the surface to cut the underbelly. The girls watched in horror as we battled the great white shark. We started to gain control with numerous stabs and gouging the eyes of the shark.

In the meantime, the girls saw a speedboat. They frantically waved it down. The boaters could see the trouble the boys were in and knew they needed to act quickly. They grabbed their spear guns and yelled out at the boys to distance themselves from the shark so they could get a clear shot at the shark. Within moments, the spear guns subdued the shark and the owners of the speedboat agreed to take us onto the beach.

We were able to purchase shovels from a little store on the beach. We then looked at the map to identify the location of the treasure. We found the designated spot and started digging, and it wasn't long before we found a huge crate. Together, we pulled the crate from the hole and opened it. We were ecstatic to see that the treasure was intact, but then discovered a note, from the Captain's log, which read "My crew and I have seen rough times. It took a lot of energy out of us when our sails snapped in half from fierce winds."

The log continued "The men were weak, and their attitude was poor, but as we journeyed on, we got stronger as we experienced better weather. Now, we find ourselves in the wake of a fierce storm. I am worried about what might happen to this treasure if our ship should sink. I hope whoever finds this loot will always respect the high seas because it has much might and wonder." As we reflected on the words of Captain Thomas Cavendish, Mr. Montgomery brought to our attention another vision by his aunt that had been passed down from generation to generation.

"My aunt, in her last several months of life, picked up visions during her meditations from an ancient past, specifically the 4th century BC. These visions were from the Nabataens, a nomadic people from a long forgotten city, offered referred to as the underground city of Petra."

The King of the Nabatean people of that era was under siege by the Roman empire; meanwhile, his daughter, who was gifted and clairvoyant, was concerned that her heritage and that of the Nabatean culture would be forgotten and she was meditating for inner peace while the Romans invaded her land and people. Mr. Montgomery went on to tell us that the king and his daughter were unceremoniously slaughtered and their bodies were left in shallow graves.

His aunt had visions that these individuals would not be a peace until they were properly buried with the rest of their people. Mr. Montgomery asked if we could help to uncover their bodies so they could finally be laid to rest. So once again, the Lawndale Gang was back in action!

We arrived in Jordan, where The Lost City of Petra was discovered in 1812. The only way to get to Petra was by camel, so we secured camels for the final leg of our trip. While riding our camels enroute to Petra, we saw vultures menacingly circling above us, hoping for their next meal. Finally, we arrived at The Lost City of Petra and surprisingly, the entrance was unguarded, giving us free access to this vast underground city.

We tried to imagine how the Nabetean Culture lived underground for 600 years before the Romans invaded them. But our job was to find the remains of the King and his daughter. The girls spread out to explore the area. The guys looked for clues as well. We hoped the King and his daughter found comfort with each other amidst the ruthless Romans and were buried together.

At last, we discovered a ditch sufficiently large to conceal bodies, leading us to speculate that this could be the site of their abandonment. It wasn't long before we unearthed the remains of the king, alongside the skeleton of his daughter. The king had a necklace around his neck that represented his royalty. We said the Lord's Prayer, removed the bones with dignity, and put them in our sacks to transport them safely so they could ultimately have a proper burial.

Mr. Montgomery wrote about these incidents in a local newspaper, which is how he remembered the Lawndale Gang. "Together, you are strong; your love for one another is your glue for your connection to life experiences, which is your compass in life. But this rule will only be effective if you believe in yourself. Keep the faith, hope, and your convictions alive, for I will never forget your efforts on my behalf."

Let Freedom Ring

We were at Penn's Landing in Philadelphia, home to a collection of ships from the past on display, and a concert stage that is often alive with the sounds of festive music. On this day, everyone was enjoying a Blues concert when we overheard what appeared to be Russian Navy soldiers bragging about how they avoided the U.S. security nets and could dock their submarine at Penn's Landing without any attention in the middle of the night. We were alarmed, so we followed them. They returned to their submarine, and it looked like they were going through their procedures to take off. "What should we do," we asked ourselves.

My brother, who was a nuclear machinist mate and a former helmsman of his submarine, a Los Angeles Class Fast Attack Submariner, realized there was no time to get the authorities involved because it appeared that the Russian sub was getting ready to leave port. We quickly assessed our options and realized we could board one of the World War II submarines that was on display at the pier and do so undetected. My brother knew how to open the hatch and we all boarded the submarine.

Thanks to my brother's knowledge, it didn't take long to power up the sub. We also had another former Navy veteran with us who studied calibration and radar when he served, and he manned the radar station. As the Russian sub pulled away, we had to contact the Joint Chiefs of Staff to inform them of our intentions and what we knew. There was a special phone on the sub with low-frequency abilities for deep-depth dives that allowed us to communicate with the Joint Chiefs.

At first, they were alarmed by our actions, but they realized we were patriots and believed we were doing the right thing. They told us that one of the Russian subs went rogue and they lost track of it, but now they knew where it is and were following it. The U.S. position was that since they didn't know the intentions with that nuclear submarine, it must be destroyed right away.

They asked us to continue following the Russian sub. Meanwhile, my brother knew that a World War II submarine would be easy to detect by a modern submarine and he needed to make adjustments to the propulsion system, so it would run silently and we could track them.

We investigated the cabins on the sub and found one that served as an office and had a film a projector. We looked through the desk drawers and found a film reel labeled "Top Secret - Russian Maritime Tactical Combat Maneuvers". We realized watching this film could give us a competitive edge against our adversaries. Still, a more significant concern loomed, because according to the oxygen sensor, the oxygen filtration was off.

Most of the girls had science backgrounds and they went to work reading the onboard books about oxygen filtration. As the girls worked to resolve this problem, we watched the film on Russian tactical maneuvers. We learned about the Crazy Ivan Maneuver, as practiced by the Soviet submarine commanders, which entailed a rapid 180 turn, immediately followed by activating the sonar. We left the projection room with more knowledge and more prepared.

To the girl's credit, the oxygen levels were starting to normalize, but our gauges didn't look normal. The pressure gauge inside the submarine was increasing, the deeper we dove to follow the Russian submarine. We knew the Russian submarine could descend much deeper than ours.

Suddenly, our monitors told us the Russian submarine had detected us and the crew was trying to contact us to discover our intentions. We replied that we were operating under direct orders from the U.S. government to pursue and hunt them down as long as the sub was in U.S. waters. While the Russian crew laughed at the "old bucket" we were in, we told them we would do whatever was necessary to capture them.

After a tense day, we gathered in the mess hall to debrief and unwind. We've been a closeknit group for several years and we feel most centered when we can relax and freely communicate our thoughts and feelings. We noticed in the mess hall that it was equipped with radio equipment, so we put on the radio, which helped us unwind even more. We talked about how amazing it was that music could evoke such powerful emotions and how music transcended all races which helped with peace and harmony. As the music started to pulsate, we began to loosen up, and suddenly, we were dancing and having fun with each other well into the night.

We woke up the following day to discover the Russian submarine was preparing to enter a large deep-water cave to avoid detection. We pursued them with our limited and inexperienced crew. The Russian submarine tried to outmaneuver us in the deep-water cave as we chased them. The cavern walls were a real test for my brother, who had to rely on sonar to drive the sub. Suddenly, and without warning, we were in grave danger. A wall was discovered in the cave. In addition, a gauge indicated where the submarine was in relation to physical matter based on sonar. As my brother was navigating the sub, I monitored this gauge and could see we had only 15 seconds before impact. I shouted, "Fifteen seconds before collision!"

My brother was tapping his foot as he tried to do the exact math to turn our sub. Then with verbal force, he yelled, "Right force, Port-side!" As we listened to my brother, we felt our sub drastically turn to the right as we continued our pursuit. Alarms went off in the sub and the member who was monitoring the radar system yelled that there were mines ahead. As my brother ran over to clarify the information on the radar screen, one of the mines detonated, and it rattled our sub with such force that it shook our senses. We contacted the Joint Chiefs of Staff with the special phone onboard and they advised us to continue our pursuit and not let the Russion submarine re-enter international waters. They indicated we should use force, if necessary. They explained the mines were put in the cave to prevent Russia, Germany, and Japan from using the cave to hide from the U.S. Fleet during the World War II.

Both the Russian sub and our sub cleared the cave and re-entered the ocean. The Russian crew was getting irritated with us and the captain decided to toy with our leader. He told us we were getting on his nerves and that we needed to go home before we got hurt. We answered that we have a reputation as winners, and we don't back down from any situation.

The Russian sub broke off communication and started to maneuver into the Crazy Ivan attack mode, which we studied and prepared for in the film room. We also prepared the U.S. counter move, which was to clear the baffles. We could see the Russian sub repositioning itself in front of us, directly locked on our position. But we weren't going to wait for them to attack us. My brother yelled for "hard rudder right, stern forward, fire torpedo one on target!" As we heard the torpedo being launched, we waited with anticipation and then heard a huge explosion that shook our boat. My brother confirmed the destruction of the Russian sub through the telescope.

We were joyous and relieved as we embraced. We had done our patriotic duty. We felt pride similar to our Forefathers, who had a vision of liberty and freedom.

Royal Jelly

This story is about our Lawndale Gang that hung out together throughout our coming-of-age years. These stories are both fiction and non-fiction, with storytelling about our group that helped other people solve mysteries and problems, putting us on many adventures.

The Lawndale Gang was hanging out on the top field across the tracks from Lawndale in Cheltenham when they were startled by a man wearing prison stripes. He cautioned them not to be afraid of him and went on to tell them about this unknown vitamin called Royal Jelly. He explained that nurse bees secrete larvae from certain bee eggs, which they isolate so they can grow into Queen Bees. This larva is called Royal Jelly, and it has many health benefits. It is a 100 percent natural superfood. It has the power to improve your immune system, which is your body's defense against infections and diseases, and helps reduce inflammation.

This prisoner said he knows of a bee farm in South Georgia where they produce the purest Royal Jelly. The farm needs help to bring its product to the market.

We agreed to help him and we jumped into an abandoned boxcar on an idling freight train going south on the tracks that separate Cheltenham and Lawndale. This took us to the Georgia swamp. Once there, we had to cross the swamp by boat. Unfortunately, we got entangled with a woodsmen in that area who had bad intentions. There were three of them with rifles, and they gathered us up and separated us by gender, leaving the seven girls with two woodsmen and one woodsman with the boys. The woodsmen who were guarding the girls decided to tie them up against a tree.

This was horrific to the Lawndale boys, watching their girls being treated this way. The woodsmen was taunting the Lawndale girls which angered the boys even more. The woodsman guarding the boys were not paying attention and instead, was watching his buddies taunt the girls. Suddenly, we charged the woodsman, grabbed his rifle, and quickly aimed it at the other two woodsmen and said, "Make another remark about our girls, and we'll blow your head off!" The woodsmen feared for their lives and immediately ran off.

As we were departing the swamp, one of the girls was bitten by a water moccasin snake. We knew we had to get her to a doctor soon. Fortunately, the prisoner knew of a Georgia bayou backwoods doctor who was in the area and could help us. The doctor treated the Lawndale girl, and we were on our way.

As we went through the bayou, we came across an abandoned church in the middle of the woods. We were perplexed as to why there was a church out this far in the bayou, but here it was. On the side of the church, the stone inscription said 1649. It looked like the church had been through a hurricane because the crucifix on top of the steeple was lying on the ground the church, and was damaged by weather over time. What a shame it was that this beautiful Christian relic was just lying here. We knew it could be beautiful again and we wanted to preserve it. Fortunately, one of our guys owned a scrap metal company and he agreed to send a team down from Philadelphia to pick up the crucifix. We wanted to hang it in our fort, to represent our strong faith that carried us through our many advantages.

Then, we wandered through the church grounds and found the graveyard associated with the church. We looked around the gravestones and found the Pastor's resting place. We noticed what seemed to be four decimals carved into a stone attached to a string in the bottom left-hand corner. What did this mean, we asked ourselves. We pondered this with many scenarios, but we decided to go back into the church and count the pews from the altar, so that's what we did.

After counting the rows of pews from the altar, we sat at the fourth pew, looking around for another clue, but didn't find anything. We noticed a slight crease on the bench. We lifted the bench and found a note. "If you have found this note, you have figured out the Inca Numerical code on my gravestone. I was the pastor of this church, but my blood is half Inca. Whoever finds this, please help me bring to the forefront my heritage's values. The Inca virtues have included strong work ethic, social equality, advanced engineering skills, and a strict moral code centered around honesty and determination. And if you

63

accomplish these things during your time on Earth, you will go peacefully into the afterlife."

We agreed to help the pastor once we got home to ensure his legacy was not lost. Then we turned our attention to the bee farm. On our way, we found an abandoned mine shaft, so we entered it. We found helmets, picks, wooden support beams, and a large pool of underground, crystal-clear natural spring water with natural minerals and electrolytes. We thought about what a great opportunity it could be to make the Royal Jelly even purer. We left the mine shaft, inspired with hope.

As we continued towards the farm, we came upon a psychic who gave us a group evaluation and warned us that trouble was ahead in our travels. We didn't know what that meant, but we remembered hearing as we grew up that we should only worry about the challenges of today and not concern ourselves with future problems. But just to be safe, we all purchased Saint Christopher necklaces from the psychic for good luck.

When we were about five miles from the bee farm, we discovered we needed to travel by horse and buggy for these last few miles. While we were in town arranging transportation with the Amish who owned the buggy company, the local authorities apprehended the prisoner who was traveling with us. He had escaped from jail to share this message about the Royal Jelly. Fortunately, before he was taken back to prison, he shared the final directions with us, so we could find our way to the bee farm.

As we were riding down the path, a group of hoodlums stopped our buggy and started to harass the Amish. They felt the Amish were an easy target because they lived a simple life and were non-confrontational. They intended to rob the Amish and their passengers, but the Lawndale boys, who were always ready to stand up to bullies, got out of the buggy and confronted the hoodlums. They immediately backed down and dispersed.

We finally arrived at the bee farm, and it was fascinating how the owners took such pride in creating the Royal Jelly. We told the owners of the natural spring source in the mine and the wheels were put into motion to extract it. We assisted the owners getting their product featured on social media and helped them build a marketing plan with a web page so people around the world could enjoy the health benefits of Royal Jelly.

Royal jelly is a widely unknown vitamin that can improve your wellbeing. It is a 100 percent superfood vitamin that is highly nutritious and bioactive and can reduce cholesterol and improve your immune system. We are proud that we helped this Royal Jelly Farm so this product could be available to so many people.

Good Must Prevail
Over Evil

As summer was coming to an end, we started planning a vacation we would take in the fall. In the meantime, one of the girls experienced a spiritual dark side of the night. In this real phenomenon, a person can go through a deep introspection and potential transformation, which can ultimately lead to a more profound spiritual awakening and leave that person with an etheric vision. There are numerous kinds of energies around us, and most people don't see them, but a person with etheric vision can see the different types of energies around us.

After doing some research, we booked a cabin in the Poconos, which was reasonable and accommodating for us, so we proceeded to navigate in that area. When we arrived, we found the cabin to be beautiful and with a wood-burning fireplace, but it had just one large bedroom with bunk beds. The rental agency had a property manager who did odds and ends for them, and he opened the house for us. He was clairvoyant who understood dark impressions and knew when he was in the presence of someone very spiritual.

The Lawndale Gang went to bed after an evening of fun. During the night, the girl who had the spiritual awakening began to experience pain in her left shoulder. She got out of bed to rub her shoulder, but the pain persisted. She was suspicious because the soreness was a nagging sensation, so she stopped, tried to relax, and focused her etheric vision on the energies of the room, and to her shock, she saw an energy beam coming from one of the drawers. She investigated and found a black purse with eight silver coins from the 17th and 18th centuries.

She woke up the rest of the Lawndale Gang from their bunk beds and shared with them what she discovered. They were in disbelief and wondered why there was a purse in the drawer with eight silver coins from so long ago. More important to consider was the energy resonance from the coins attacking the girl with etheric vision. We knew this was some Black Magic, but who would do this? And why? We had to find a way to break the energy connection between the coins and her shoulder, as we feared the attack could lead to her heart.

We put a cup of water in the middle of the floor and prayed to God to bless it so we would have holy water, and then we emptied out a room deodorant bottle and replaced it with the holy water. We placed the purse in the middle of the floor, and sprayed the holy water until the energy resonation was finally cut. We returned to our beds, wondering who had done this.

The next morning, we sat in the living room, discussing what had transpired the night before. The girl who was blessed with etheric vision saw something odd in the eyes of one of the people in a photograph on top of the entertainment center in the room. She moved in for a closer look and to her dismay, discovered the picture was of an older woman, whose eyes looked very alive but filled with a strange energy. It was so unusual she called to the rest of the Lawndale Gang to get a closer look and see if they could see what she observed, even though they didn't have the same etheric vision. Most saw a small glimmer of this energy and began asking, "What's going on? How did this energy get into the old lady's eyes?"

As we tried to understand what was happening, the maintenance man from the rental agency arrived. He had a way of staring at us that was very disconcerting. We noticed that he was in one of the photos on the entertainment center, because his family often stayed at the cabin. We looked closer at his picture and saw a Pentagram for a necklace. Without notice, the man rushed to the drawer where the black purse had been found, as if he knew the energy was cut off. He was clearly upset, but realized he couldn't accuse the Lawndale Gang of disrupting the coins, or it would quickly incriminate him and he would need to provide an explanation.

One of the members of the Lawndale Gang lit a candle to establish a calmer mood amongst the group. It didn't take long for the girl with the etheric vision to notice that evil energy was emanating from the candle. She brought this to our attention, but the maintenance man quickly responded, "You're wrong, there's no evil energy coming from that candle!"

We knew right away something was amiss in this cabin and the maintenance man likely held the answers. It was time for us to start investigating the situation.

We immediately looked up a highly credentialed White Witch in the area to get some answers. White Witches only deal with white light, which resonates with God. We explained everything we had been through with the coins, the candles, and the picture of the maintenance man wearing a Pentagram around his neck. The White Witch suggested that he may use the Pentagram to access dark energy and could use his black magic against us. Pentagrams are usually used for good intentions, but it is possible to use them for dark purposes. The witch advised us that if he was proficient in dark energy, we must bring him before the altar at the Church of Archangel Gabriel, near Peace Valley Lake in Mount Pocono. As we returned back to the cabin to discuss how to accomplish this, the maintenance man arrived, wanting to know what we had done with the coins from the purse.

He confronted us and told us that the coins had been in his family for 400 years and they were very important to him. The girls exclaimed, "Those coins were being used for evil purposes! You were the reason our friend felt such pain in her shoulder."

The man responded "I despise her depth of spirituality and I'm here to let her know that my beliefs are superior." Immediately one of the girls responded, "It's sad that you think your beliefs are stronger than our faith, which has unlimited Divine Power." The guys then grabbed him, subdued him and brought him to the Church of Archangel Gabriel.

As we arrived at the church, we dragged the man to the altar and placed him under the suspended crucifix. As we did this, he cried out to his dark forces for help, but we intervened and prayed to God, with him under the suspended crucifix, to help us. Then we saw a beam of white energy come through the crucifix and onto the head of the man. At first, he tried to shake off God's intervention, but finally, God's Grace prevailed, and the man started to cry because he knew that the power of God had touched him and saved him.

We all left the church as one and felt honored that this opportunity fell into our path, because we know our faith is bountiful and has no limits.

Sinbad the Sailor

A renowned author of books about Sinbad contacted us and explained she was always intrigued by whether the mystical side of Sinbad was true or not. She said that she had written many books, but never had actually followed the evidence for its veracity on the mystical end. She wanted us to unravel that for her.

We agreed on all the details and as a group, decided to embark on this trip using a sailboat and the best nautical locations of Sinbad's destinations. We rented a sailboat leaving from Penn's Landing, and we followed the map of Sinbad's most famous voyages.

Our destination was the Great Barrier Reef, where we understood Sinbad landed on many islands in ancient times. While following Sinbad's exact route, we experienced strange atmospheric conditions. This included swirling winds and choppy waves that rocked our boat. We heard howling winds and we were terrified to see ghostly witches on broomsticks circling our sailboat, warning us not to go further. We've always believed that confronting our fears brings the greatest rewards, so we chose to continue our journey, despite the warnings. Suddenly, we went through a variance that sent us back in time. We knew this because the birds in the sky looked prehistoric, and certainly not like any birds we had ever seen before.

We arrived at a deserted island near the Great Barrier Reef in Australia and brought supplies from the boat to help us survive. Once settled, the boys made sturdy wooden walking sticks and spears to help explore the island. To our surprise, we discovered the initials STS on a tree near the beach, which we were sure stood for Sinbad the Sailor.

The girls gathered firewood, while the boys pitched the tents for the night and built a suspended fire pit for cooking the meat we hoped to catch with our spears. We then collected seashells that the girls could use to decorate the campsite. While we were out collecting seashells, the girls got stuck in quicksand and cried out for help. We hurried down the path towards the screams and found them sinking into quicksand up to their armpits. We had to do something quickly; these were our girls, and they had been with us through thick and thin! We found nearby sturdy branches and threw them out to the girls to grab. We then pulled them to safety one by one. After the last girl was rescued, we shared a group hug filled with love and continued our activities into the night.

We spent the night by the fire on the beach, enjoying good company and laughter, and by morning, we were ready to get back to work. We began by surveying the island and checking out the numerous paths. As we were walking along one path, large bats appeared. There were attacking us, so we had to run down the path to escape, only to discover it led right to the edge of a cliff. Fortunately, we had packed nylon and a cliff anchor, so one of the guys hurled the nylon across the ridge until it reached the other side. We made the connection tight and started to carefully cross the nylon beam to safety on the other side. As the last girl was crossing, a giant pterodactyl suddenly swooped down, grabbed her with its claws, and flew away.

We were shocked and horrified as one of the boys shouted, "Did you see the wingspan on that bird? It had to be 20 feet." Another Lawndale boy said, "No, it was 24 feet long!" The next Lawndale boy said, "I think it was 28 feet long!" We were in shock as we saw the pterodactyl fly alongside the cliff to a huge nest. We gathered our rope to rappel down to our friend. As we climbed, we noticed rocks crumbling beneath us, but kept the nest in sight. Once we reached the nest, several of the boys rappelled down into the nest, but as we were rappelling, one of the pterodactyl eggs was hatching. We knew from our own past, chicks that hatch are normally hungry, and these eggs were about three feet in diameter. Our girl was vulnerable in that nest.

We reached the nest and quickly rescued our girl, lifting her to safety just before the pterodactyl egg hatched. Once we reached the top of the cliff, we found another pathway back to our campsite on the beach. Along the way, we found an old shack adjacent to the path and decided to search it for possible clues. While searching, we found a crate with the initials STS on it, so we opened it and found brandy. This must have been Sinbad's brandy, and we agreed to bring a few bottles back to the campsite. The girls collected firewood for the campfire. Between the

73

brandy and the campfire, our nerves relaxed, and we enjoyed each other's company with laughter and heartfelt conversations. We split into teams for a fun night of charades before going to bed.

We rose in the morning and were keeping ourselves busy around the campsite when several of the boys saw something out in the surf. It had a large fin, so we got on our boat to explore. As we approached, we realized it was a mermaid, beckoning to us to come closer. We paddled closer until she was beside our boat.

"I am Athena the Mermaid, and I have been swimming along the Barrier Reef for many years. I am here to help you, since you are in great danger. Sinbad used to visit this island a long time ago. He was special and would ride the pterodactyl with confidence. Beware of the Evil Witch; she can summon the fire-breathing dragon from the ocean and raise skeletons to do her bidding. They'll come out of the Cave of the Evil Past. But I'm here to help. Go west one mile past the cliff and you'll find a waterfall. At the base of the waterfall, there's a metal crate containing armor to shield you from the dragon's fire and the skeletons."

We thanked Athena profusely, and she gave us a final message. "I wish you luck in your pursuit of the truth. Allow that goal to drive you towards your destiny." And Athena was off. We realized how blessed we were that she helped us as we paddled towards the shore. We told the girls what the mermaid told us, as we were concerned about what lie ahead for us on our journey.

We reached the waterfalls and dove into the water, where we found a large crate with armor. We retrieved it to prepare for battle against the dragons and skeletons. As we were walking down the path towards our campsite, the Evil Witch appeared and threatened us.

"I'm the Evil Witch of the island. State your purpose here."

One of the girls stepped forward and said bravely, "We were hired by an author to authenticate whether this island was mystical."

The witch leaned forward and said, "You must know by now that it is, and I don't want the outside world to know that. So beware, I'm going to stop you at all cost."

The Lawndale girl replied that she could try, but our group believed good must prevail over evil. The witch shook her head as she exclaimed, "You foolish mortals with your lofty ideals, I will crush you."

The Lawndale girl quickly replied, "If the idea is born in truth, we know there is infinite power there." The witch was obviously insulted and took off.

We continued walking down the path and suddenly, from beyond the brush, ten life-sized skeletons with swords were ordered out of a cave by the Evil Witch. We were caught off guard as they rushed us with great force. The girls stood behind us as the boys attempted to fight off the skeletons, but they only had their walking sticks to defend themselves. The boys bravely fought back despite being outnumbered ten to nine.

Meanwhile, the girls devised a plan to distract the skeletons away from the boys. The skeletons chased the girls into the forest, but the girls led them into the quicksand. The boys caught up with the girls as we watched the skeletons sink into the quicksand, while the Evil Witch flew overhead, gazing down at us in anger.

We reached our campsite and prepared for another night of kinship as we lit the campfire to relax and eat dinner. We decided to play "Would You Rather," where one person in the group would present two hypothetical situations, each person would choose the option they prefer and state the reason behind their answer. We played this into the night with much merriment and fun.

The next morning, we learned that the Evil Witch had summoned a fire-breathing dragon, but we didn't know where it would appear. Suddenly, the dragon with its mammoth wings came into view from the ocean. The dragon's deep, resonating roar alerted us to the danger upon us. We grabbed our armor and spears to prepare for battle. The boys attacked the dragon from different angles, while its fierce fire bounced off the armor. One of the Lawndale boys climbed onto the dragon and used a rope to hold it, but the dragon violently shook its head to throw him off.

Meanwhile, the other Lawndale boys continued fighting the dragon. The dragon recognized the resiliency in their actions and recognized that he didn't want to continue to be under the power of the Evil Witch. He slowly started to calm down and finally lowered his head in acknowledgement to the source of strength at the core of the Lawndale gang. The dragon then allowed the Lawndale gang to pet him with affection to let them know that they had his respect. He then returned to the ocean.

Our job was done, and we had plenty of information for the author who hired us, as we prepared our sailboat to return home. Collectively we went to the front of the sailboat and one of the girls proclaimed to the Evil Witch, "We leave here with our quest done and we hope you learned the lesson of true power. When your intentions are anchored and your thoughts motivated by love, then you can move mountains."

We set sail with the good mermaid on the port side and the dragon on the starboard side guiding us towards home.

The Legacy of Kokopelli

This story is both fiction and nonfiction with some storytelling.

The Lawndale Gang needed a vacation, so we reserved an inn for five days in Rehoboth Beach, Delaware. It was two blocks from the beach, and two blocks from all the quaint and alternative spiritual shops on Main Street. After walking on the boardwalk, we visited the shops. We walked into one shop that had figures behind the register that were about 18 inches high. We inquired about them, and the store owner explained that it was a figure of of Kokopelli. We said, "Who was he?"

The merchant explained that Kokopelli was a very inspirational person who lived around 750 BCE and was a Navajo Indian from the southwestern United States. The folklore was that he was a storyteller to the children and adults of the villages he visited and played his music on his flute to entertain people. He was very spiritual and played his flute for a bountiful harvest for the villagers, and that's why they called him a fertility spirit; they believed he helped them with their harvest.

We found the above picture of Kokopelli in a book in the shop. The merchant went on to tell us that there was a hate group trying to suppress the inspirational story of Kokopelli, because of its positive impact.

They were the Nazi Swastika Party, who also participated in the Arts of Dark Matter. We decided it would be our mission to bring attention to this folklore hero and protect his legacy from the Nazi Swastika Party.

As we left his shop with a cause and purpose, we decided to go to a fortune teller on the same block who was famous in Rehoboth Beach for her accuracy. We told her of our intentions, and she looked deep into our fortunes and told us that a strong malevolent force was against us.

"Don't forget to pray often, but let me remind you that you're in one of the most-renowned shore towns that gives people a renewal of energy with the natural elements that are down here. Please take advantage of them," said the fortune teller. Then she gave us a list of items that would help us achieve our mission.

First, we purchased a large seashell from the sea shell shop just down the street. Then we bought a shiva lingam stone. Shiva lingam stones are naturally formed over millions of years from the Narmada River. They are composed of various minerals, such as basalt, jasper, and quartz, giving them distinctive appearance and power. Villagers remove the stones from the river, polish them, and perform holy blessings on them. The fortune teller also advised us to go to the beach and gather as many of the crystalized pebbles that wash up in the surf. She explained these crystalized stones are formulated by sand compressed with pebbles, crystalized, and polished by the ocean. Collectively, they can harness incredible power as a natural resource. We then purchased a dozen blessed reiki candles to burn, as they were supposed to grant us good karma in pursuing our cause. The last item on the list was from the African Shop on Main Street. Male elephant ivory tusks are known through African folklore as a deterrent to evil energy because of the might and power of elephants.

The fortune teller had instructed us to take all these items to a prayer group that met daily. She explained that the group would ask for blessings to give us stamina, strength, and protection. We knew how important it was to bring the story of Kokopelli to life, because it was so inspirational.

The Nazi Swastika Party was summoning up evil entities in an attempt to stop us. We went about our travels, continued educating ourselves on Kokopelli, and found an ancient article explaining his existence. On many walls in the American Southwest, which were more than 3000 years ago, we saw a figure of a humpbacked flute player called Kokopelli—a person who visited villages and interceded on their behalf. He prayed and played his flute for it to rain, so the villagers would have a good harvest. He would help to change the winter to spring. The depiction of the pottery and petroglyphs of Kokopelli goes back to 700 BCE, and they say his humpback is depicted because he is carrying seeds and stories for the villagers. Villagers would sing and dance throughout the night while he played the flute. Kokopelli was legendary for making music, telling stories, helping bring better crops, and as a source of dancing and joy to those around him.

We felt honored to help bring Kokopelli's legacy to the surface, so people could see what a great man he was. We were concerned about what the fortune teller told us, but were entrenched in our faith. We also knew that in all faith, some trials and sacrifices work toward a bigger plan set forth by God.

We decided to have a picnic one day and drove until we came upon an abandoned farmhouse with lots of farmland. We set out our picnic, so we could relax and enjoy each other's company. Suddenly, we noticed several energy sources that looked transparent, but had form to them. They looked sinister, and we could see an energy resonation streaming from the energy source and starting to attack us, which was very painful. All of us began to become inflicted with intense pain from the devasting attack from the sinister entities. We fell to the ground, trying to recover from the attack.

When we saw the girls in pain, the leader of our group said, "From the depths of my soul, I oppose evil with all my might and being. I feel the balance of good and evil has been given to us to prevail. We fought a good fight, but now we fear we are losing. From the greatness of God's infinite power, please protect us." We looked at our car. Inside the car were the shiva lingam stone, elephant ivory tusks, the seashells, crystalized pebbles and the reiki candles. We saw a beam of energy come from our car, and it started to engage the sinister energy beings and chase them away. We were in awe and thankful for the heavenly response to our request.

As we returned to our inn, we reflected on our journey and the knowledge that when you trust your good intentions, positive elements unravel that impact your landscape with resounding ramifications. We sensed that a Godly system is at play whenever you live with a forward-looking attitude. We celebrated that evening with a trip to a karaoke bar, where we sang our favorite songs and celebrated our friendship.

The following day, before we returned home, we visited the beach one last time to watch the sun rise. We stood hand in hand, facing the sun, and thought about how we have learned that through opportunities, the potential of the human spirit is bountiful, because God's universe has no limits.

The Cornerstone of our Country

It was time for us to plan our next vacation and we decided this time; we wanted to include a bit of history about the early days of our country. So, we planned a trip to Philadelphia, the birthplace of our Constitution. We reserved rooms at a bed & breakfast in this historic city, one that was converted from a 1700s inn and where George Washington and Thomas Jefferson are said to have stayed while shaping our nation. We started the day with an historic tour of Philadelphia, beginning at Christ Church at 2nd and Market Street.

Our tour guide was very informative, telling us that George Washington, John Adams, Benjamin Franklin, and Betsy Ross were among the residents of the great city of Philadelphia. The tour guide revealed that a rifle belonging to George Washington has never been found, and what happened to it is still a mystery. Christ Church is the site of colonial America's break with England and the birthplace of the American Episcopal Church.

The tour guide went on to explain that there were tunnels underneath the church that were 200 ft. long and started beneath the steeple where the bells were rung. Bells rang for various reasons, symbolizing historic events like Victory Day and Remembrance Day, and calling people to worship. The tour guide informed us that during the British invasion of Philadelphia, church bells were hidden in tunnels and moved to Allentown, where they were submerged in the Delaware River for safe keeping until after the war.

We returned to our bed & breakfast, settled in the living room, and lit a cozy fire in the fireplace. We reflected on the lives of the brave thinkers who dared to challenge the King of England, who sought to control and heavily tax the colonists. Then we moved on and decided to play "Never have I ever," a drinking game we have played before and brought much laughter. The first player of the game says a statement that starts with "Never have I ever" and describes something they have never done. The player takes a sip of a drink when the player says an action that the group can challenge for its veracity. We had fun late into the night and afterwards went to our beds.

The next day, we visited the Betsy Ross House, where she reportedly met George Washington to discuss making the first American flag. The tour guide told us Thomas Jefferson wrote the Declaration of Independence in a small boarding house on Market Street. He also mentioned that the pen Jefferson used was hidden somewhere in Monticello, his home near Charlottesville, Virginia. But apparently, no one knows exactly where this pen is located.

After visiting the Betsy Ross House, we had lunch and talked about how significant it would be for our country if we could find George Washington's rifle and Thomas Jefferson's pen.

We visited Thomas Jefferson's boarding house at 7th and Market St, where he wrote the Declaration of Independence on the second floor. We were surprised at how small the quarters were. The house had some artifacts behind a glass partition, and one of them was his hat. When the security guard was distracted, one of the boys sneaked behind the glass partition to check his hat for any helpful clues for our quest. He didn't have much time, so he tried to be respectful of the hat while looking for any clues. He discovered a note in the hat's lining that read, "What is always at the center of everything, but can never be touched?" He took the note, and we went to a coffee shop to discuss its meaning. What could it mean?

We discovered that Jefferson's study was located at the center of his home in Monticello, Virginia. Perhaps the very pen that was used to write the Declaration of Independence is housed in the study. We took a bus to Charlottesville, for a walking tour of Monticello. Once at Monticello, we turned our attention to his study. We sat at his actual desk to imagine what life was like for him back in the day. We pulled out his desk drawer, looked around, and felt underneath the drawer. Sure enough, there was a small package, which we opened. We were amazed to discover the actual pen he wrote the Declaration of Independence with, which had 56 signers from the Continental Congress.

We were very proud of ourselves for making this important discovery. We donated it to the Monticello Museum, so current and future generations of

Americans could see it for themselves when touring Jefferson's home in Virginia.

On the bus ride home, we sat at the back of the bus and talked about our forefathers who built this country. Many of them were slave owners, but they were brilliant at how they put the principles, laws and building blocks in place for our nation to grow. As President Obama stated, the Constitution is a living document that should be understood in the context of a changing world. This means that the Constitution was designed to expand with the growing needs of the government.

We arrived back at the bed and breakfast, gathered around a roaring fire, and engaged in a lively discussion about the Constitutional Convention. From what we understood, each state sent two delegates to the Constitutional Convention to develop a constitution for the government. The key to our thriving economy lies in the Constitution, particularly the right to engage in commerce, which is essential for a free market that benefits us all. We recognized our forefathers were true visionaries in many ways and we owe so much to them.

While tending the fire, the fire poker got stuck in something beneath the logs. One of the boys tried to get it loose, but with no success. Finally, he gathered his strength and pulled one last time, only to unearth something beneath the fire logs. He took a closer look and saw that a ceramic panel had come loose, and we waited for the fire to burn down before checking it out.

We moved the fire logs aside and uncovered a raised ceramic tile. After removing it, we discovered an old ramrod from a revolutionary rifle, used to push projectiles into a muzzle-loading gun. The initials on the ramrod were G.W. We were shocked at our discovery. Could this possibly be the ramrod belonging to George Washington? We recalled the tour guide at Christ Church mentioning that George Washington's rifle had never been found.

We looked around the living room for clues but couldn't find any. On display in the dining room was an old set of shoes that were said to belong to George Washington. They were separated by a glass partition, yet still within reach. We carefully inspected the shoes, hoping to find a clue.

We found a riddle on the tongue of one of the shoes that read, "As I melt away, the more meaning I have. The more I'm used, the thinner I show, duration helps me. Where is my rifle?" We concluded that this riddle was about ice, so we started reading about ice and its usage back in colonial times. Icehouses were separate from main houses and were insulated with large concrete blocks. We concluded that the Betsy Ross House might have had an icehouse, and George Washington visited several times, while she was sewing the American flag.

We immediately paid a visit to the Betsy Ross House, and as we had guessed, it had an icehouse. But we didn't know how we could get around the security guards. They happened to be female security guards, so we picked what we thought were the two best looking guys in our group to flirt with them. Once we knew they were distracted, we went to the icehouse. It was locked, but one of our members had learned from his locksmith father how to pick a lock with a paperclip. After numerous attempts, he unlocked the padlock, and we gained entry to the empty icehouse. The key phrase that was in the riddle was "duration helps me." We thought this might be referring to the concrete because the insulation would slow the process of thawing. So, we looked closely at the concrete slabs that shaped the icehouse for a clue.

We looked around thoroughly, removing small pieces of stone and concrete. Then we unearthed a rifle sling from the Revolutionary War days, and on the leather strapping were the initials F.O.O.C. This perplexed us for a while, but we finally put the words together, "Father of Our Country." We got excited and started to move the slabs around in that area, eventually revealing George Washington's rifle. We were so relieved that we found this important artifact for history's sake.

Our journey to historic Philadelphia was over, and we were thankful for the opportunities that were presented to us. We learned that before our government was created in 1776, no government was like the one our forefathers created. It's clear that they drew inspiration from spiritual literature when shaping the foundations of this country.

The Living Force
of Star Wars

The *Star Wars* film saga was one of the biggest franchises in movie-making history. It blends adventure with spiritual themes through the concept of the "Force". The film franchise, consisting of nine films explored universal questions about good versus evil, and the balance of power between light and dark. *Star Wars* is known for its adventure and the Jedi's ability to tap into the "Force", but it also offers valuable spiritual teachings that can help humanity grow.

A historian, who was also a big *Star Wars* fan, reached out to us to highlight the spiritual teachings of Star Wars. He believes these teachings will help people see the similarities between the "Force" and God's Universe, highlighting the values and principles that lead humanity to enlightenment. Star Wars spirituality draws from Middle Eastern philosophies and has roots in Sanskrit, which reflects ancient teachings that predate both Hinduism and Buddhism. The doctrines advocate that there is a force in the universe that is beneficial to humanity.

Over time, we had built a reputation like the Hardy Boys and Nancy Drew for going on adventures and solving mysteries. The historian explained that a group known as the Vikings of the Old Order believed its historical events were misrepresented by the *Star Wars* saga. They think that a Jedi Knight's lightsaber is a copy of their traditional swords. They believed the Star Wars franchise would be stronger if people understood the spiritual power presented in the films could uplift humanity. The historian explained that the Vikings of the Old Order had a psychic in their group for guidance.

The Lawndale Group had explored the *Star Wars* saga and discovered that true power lies in intellectual capabilities, crucial for unleashing the mind's potential. Unlocking the power of the mind reinforces the importance of recognizing the significance and scale of the material world in which we live. The scope of the material world is immeasurable in relation to what you can achieve when you believe. Nothing is impossible for you!

The Vikings of the Old Order were upset to learn that the Lawndale Group was trying to revive the Star Wars saga by emphasizing its spirituality, and they were determined to stop us. They planned to intercept the Lawndale Gang to capture and punish them because they were a hateful group that longed for the violent past of their history.

The Lawndale Gang decided to attend a movie at the Crest Theater in Lawncrest, which was a neighborhood adjacent to Lawndale. After the movie, we took a seldom-used exit that led us into an alley, and brought us out to Rising Sun Ave. We stepped into the alley and saw that the Vikings of the Old Order were waiting for us and clearly outnumbered us. The boys told the girls to take shelter while they assessed the situation, realizing a big fight was about to ensue.

The Vikings of the Old Order took out their switchblades, leaving the boys defenseless. They quickly looked around and grabbed wooden debris and trash can lids for protection. Although the boys were outnumbered, they held their own against the switchblades using what they had.

The girls went back to the theater and, after waiting for the crowd to exit, quickly got into their cars. They jumped the curb with their vehicles and drove down the alley, speeding past the Viking group to help the boys. The girls yelled at the boys "Get In," and the Lawndale Gang took off together. But in our hearts, we knew that turmoil was ahead, as we continued our journey.

We took a day to relax and enjoy a music festival at Penn's Landing. It was the Jambalaya Jam, a festival of grassroots Louisiana music. Before we knew it, the Vikings of the Old Order arrived and were even larger in number than the day before. We knew we had to protect the girls, so we urgently looked around Penn's Landing to find a place they would be safe. We saw a replica of a Leif Erikson sailboat on display with a staff to operate it. This was an actual sailboat used for Leif Erikson Cereal and it was used as goodwill ambassador by the makers of Dairy Sun Makers to promote their cereal. The sailboat travels from port to port promoting the product. We boarded the sailboat and informed the staff of our urgent situation. They agreed to help us escape from the Vikings.

Once out in the open sea, we convinced staff to replicate the maiden voyage of Columbus to South America. The staff anticipated that it would take four days to sail down to South America. On the first night, the Lawndale Gang was in awe of the celestial body of stars in the sky. One of our members amazed us by recalling the connection between the mind and the stars, sharing insights from her reading.

She explained how positive thoughts in our minds transcend time and space to help us move forward with our life. We saw the Big Dipper, a group of seven stars in the Northern Hemisphere, and wondered about it.

The next day, two of the boys climbed the masts to the top and yelled, and yelled, "Humpback Whales on starboard side!" Everyone made their way to the right-hand side of the ship to find two beautiful, 30-foot humpback whales. It was a breathtaking experience to witness nature's most remarkable treasures up close. As night fell, we discovered the sailboat had an advanced stereo system. We tuned in to a dance station on the radio and enjoyed dancing together under the open sky, having a great time on the high seas.

During the next day, we realized for us to move forward in peace, we needed to sit down with the Vikings of the Old Order, and see what their real issues were. We hoped to clear up any misunderstandings, so we could all move forward with life. We thought this was the best way to handle the issue. Nighttime descended on us, and we decided to play poker into the night with lots of gamesmanship and strategy. This turned out to be the perfect distraction for us. With two of the boys on the mast the next day, they saw the land of Venezuela, South America, where Columbus discovered America. We were delighted to take Columbus's maiden voyage to South America, but now we had to focus on getting home.

After we arrived home, we hired a lawyer and set up a meeting with the Vikings group to discuss our differences. Their main concern was that the Jedi Knights' lightsabers too closely resembled the swords belonging to the Vikings of the Old Order. Our delegation explained that a Jedi Knight lightsaber is a plasma blade powered by a diatium power cell and Jedi Knights were guardians of the universe. The *Star Wars* saga explores the duality between good and evil, and we recognized the pride in their heritage. This will always be the fabric of life as people pursue their choices.

We proposed viewing the sword as a foundational element of the lightsaber, symbolizing humanity's need to evolve. We pointed out that the sword and lightsaber should complement each other, rather than conflict, working together for a greater purpose
We all left with our principles intact for a better future to prosper.

We can learn valuable spiritual lessons from the *Star Wars* saga, such as Master Yoda's message that a peaceful mind leads to clearer and better decision-making. He also emphasized how we are luminous beings, with energy all around us that penetrates us. A Jedi Knight must have the most serious mind. This teaching is most important for anyone who wants to achieve great things!

I was a big fan of the *Star Wars* saga because it taught me a lot of values about life, and I hope this story touched you as well.

The Lawndale Gang Pursues the Secrets of Mankind

There is a story is about an explorer who was a Russian doctor named Nicholas Notovitch. In 1887, he broke his leg and stayed at a Himalayan monastery where he came across the 14 scrolls of young Jesus' teachings. According to ancient sources, Jesus had traveled to India and Tibet to preach and study between the ages of 17 to 28, before returning home to Israel to begin his ministry for God.

While the basis of this story is true and the group existed, this version is laced with fictional storytelling.

The Lawndale Gang would often watch television and one day programming was interrupted with a special news update. Apparently, pirates were trying to steal the ancient teachings of young Jesus during his time in India.

These ancient teachings, which are on scrolls in a Himalayan monastery in Tibet, are kept are kept in a

95

secret location. They can help mankind move to higher levels of spiritual consciousness. The pirates were after these ancient teachings for their own personal gain and hoped to achieve a higher power for malevolent purposes. We watched the breaking news with concern and wondered about the fate of Jesus' ancient teachings.

Our neighborhood bordered Cheltenham Township, where there was a park called Tookany Park, which had a running creek and beautiful nature path. One day, we decided to take a walk on the nature path deep into Tookany Park. As we were walking, we noticed an odd-shaped formation of rocks that looked like the strategic placement of four-foot walls that had a spiritual feel to it. They were not directly on the path, but we were curious, so we went there to explore.

As we looked around these formations of stone walls, we saw one area of the wall that was loose, so we went closer to explore and removed some loose stones. We discovered a rolled-up ancient piece of paper with some information written on it. It explained the existence of the Lenape Valley Indians who resided along the Tookany Creek during the 1650s (before the arrival of English settlers). It went on to say how the Lenape Valley Indians were ahead of their time by observing divinity in nature and how it is possible for mankind to raise its spiritual consciousness to higher levels in order to gain a higher power for enlightenment. Finally, it mentioned rumors of a great healer who would bring salvation to humanity and that he had traveled to India to get a rich, diverse understanding of the other world religions like Buddhism and Hinduism before he started his ministry.

The we were stunned by what we had read and tried to make sense of it. Obviously, the Lenape Valley Indians were referring to Lord Jesus, but we were concerned that the pirates were after the lost teachings of Jesus in India for the wrong purposes. We agreed it would be awful if the Lost Teachings of Jesus fell into the wrong hands, and we felt obligated to do something about it.

We needed to stop the pirates from gaining higher spiritual power for the wrong purposes, so each of us tapped into our college funds and traveled to India with this clue from the Lenape Valley Indians.

We landed in India, and according to the palm leaf scroll we found, Jesus traveled to Aryas, India, where he taught and studied the diversity of the world religions. When we arrived in Aryas, we learned that Jesus was only 17 years old when he taught the people of India the Holy Scriptures and how to achieve a higher power.

As we started to ask questions about the origins and authenticity of Jesus coming to India when he was 17 to study, we were directed to an wise old man who told us about the travels of young Jesus. The old man told us that Jesus traveled up to the Himalayan Mountains to study at a Buddhist temple in Tibet, where he gained a rich understanding of the Buddhism and Hindu religions before returning home to Israel at the age of 28.

Little did we know that the pirates arrived before we got there, and we learned they were well-armed. Suddenly, the pirates appeared and started to threaten the old man if he didn't reveal the secrets from Jesus on how to reach a higher power. But the old man put up a strong resistance, which inspired us to intervene. So, while the pirates were preoccupied with threatening the old man, we grabbed the chairs that were close to us and used them to attack the pirates, while they were distracted.

The pirates immediately dispersed and took up a position to gun down the Lawndale Gang, but the brave guys of the group overwhelmed the pirates before they had an opportunity to use their weapons. A fist fight ensued between the Lawndale guys and the pirates. Knowing that the Lawndale guys were younger and stronger, the pirates withdrew. They knew the next place to go to take possession of the lost teachings of Jesus was a mountain monastery on a in Tibet. The Lawndale Gang pursued them. They knew had to arrive there first to protect the lost teachings from the pirates.

As the Lawndale gang traveled to the monastery in Tibet, they learned along the way that young Jesus was known for educating the people of India. Ephesians 1:19, says, "God and his incomparably great power for us to believe. That power is the same as the mighty strength of God". And Corinthians 2:5, which reads, "So that your faith does not rest on human wisdom, but only on God's Power." We came to understand that the young Jesus taught the Holy Scriptures to enlighten the people of India with his divine knowledge.

We were in awe at the young Jesus' teachings as we continued to pursue the pirates to Tibet. Although we were learning a lot about the young Jesus, we took it upon ourselves to stop the pirates from obtaining this knowledge and let humanity be aware of these lost teachings of our Higher Power.

We journeyed far on our travels to Tibet and grew weary. We were also a bit bewildered because of the thinner air in the higher attitudes. We were gasping for air, as our energy levels were depleted enroute to the monastery. One of the members of our group was clairvoyant, and he saw from a distance a tree that seemed to have a special aura around it.

Suddenly, a form of energy appeared before us, which had wings, and said, "I am Angel Eva Marie, and I have been sent to help you during your journey. You must not give up as you are needed to protect the lost teachings of young Jesus. Let me guide you to these trees, so you can place your hands on them."

The Lawndale Gang followed the angel's instructions, and each of them placed their hands on the trunks of the trees. And then the angel gave her blessing for all trees on Earth who have great strength and wisdom to coalesce this great power and come through these selected trees to energize the Lawndale Gang members to bring them strength to carry on.

Angel Eva Marie told the Lawndale Gang that they needed to go to a Tibetan Monastery in the Himalayas to find the ancient scrolls from young Jesus, as the scrolls contained 14 chapters for higher knowledge that would benefit mankind.

The Lawndale group proceeded to the Tibetan Monastery to find the ancient scrolls before the pirates,. Unfortunately, they were too late and suddenly they were surrounded by the pirates. One bold Lawndale Gang member spoke up and said, "We're here to make sure that the integrity of young Jesus' words is not manipulated in any way." The pirates laughed and asked who would stop them, since they were well armed.

As the pirates were laughing at the impending fate of the Lawndale Gang, the boys rushed the pirates, caught them off guard and a hand-to-hand battle ensued. As the Lawndale boys were getting the upper hand in their battle with the pirates, the pirates suddenly pulled out switchblades and made the Lawndale boys retreat. As they retreated, they found large ceramic vases close by, which they picked up and ran to the pirates. The Lawndale boys crashed the large ceramic vases over the heads of the pirates, causing them to retreat and allowing the Lawndale Gang to continue on their journey.

The group successfully retrieved the 14 lost scrolls of young Jesus, and as they read some of the ancient text, they were in awe of the words written by such a young man. Here are some of the highlights of young Jesus' words:

"The eternal Judge, who is God, the eternal Spirit, constitutes the one and only soul of the universe, and it is this soul alone which creates, contains and revives all."

"He alone has willed and created. He alone has existed from eternity, and Jesus' existence will be without end; there is no one like Him either in the Heavens or on Earth."

"The great Creator has divided His power with no other being, far less with inanimate objects, as you have been taught to believe, for He alone is Omnipotent and all-sufficient."

"He willed, and the world was. By one divine thought, He has put under the power of man, the lands, the waters, the beasts, and everything which he created, and which He himself preserves in immutable order, allotting to each its proper duration."

"Even as a father shows kindness towards his children, so will God judge men after death, in conformity with His merciful laws. He will never humiliate His child by casting His soul for chastisement into the body of a beast."

The Lawndale Gage was so inspired by the young Jesus' words they went outside to watch the sun rise, and put their hands together on their chests as if to pray. As the sun came up over the mountains, they worshiped Jesus and prayed for inspiration and guidance.

According to the scrolls, young Jesus then left the Himalayan Mountains, descended into the valley of Radjipoutan Village, and headed toward the West, preaching to the people the Supreme perfection attainable by man. And the good he must do to his fellow man, which is the surest means of union with the eternal Spirit. "He who has recovered his primitive purity," said young Jesus. "Shall die with his transgressions forgiven and have the right to contemplate the majesty of God."

As we left the Himalayan Mountains, we followed the Lord Jesus' steps as he returned home to Israel to prepare for start of His Ministry at the age of 30, and the Power of Forgiveness Blessed by God for the people of Israel and for all generations to come with God.

The Ark of the Covenant

We were all hanging on our corner at Magee and Oakley in Lawndale, when a mysterious man approached us, delivered a package, and walked away into the evening dusk.

We opened up the package, and it was an invitation to the mansion of a wealthy antiquities owner in Doylestown, Pennsylvania. So, we decided to accept this invitation and when we arrived we were escorted to dinner with our host providing us a history lesson on the last whereabouts of the Ark of the Covenant. According to the host, the chronology of the Ark of the Covenant's whereabouts, according to biblical and historical accounts, spans from its creation during the exodus from Egypt to its disappearance after the Babylonian conquest of Jerusalem.

The Ark was constructed by Moses following God's instructions and was housed within the portable Tabernacle. It accompanied the Israelites for 40 years during their wilderness journeys. After the Israelites enter Canaan, the Ark was moved to Shiloh, which became a religious center for the tribes of Israel. The Israelites brought the Ark to the battle of Eben-Ezer, hoping for victory, but the Philistines captured it. Its chronology ended there.

Professor Hutchison who is a curator at one of the museums in Doylestown hired the Lawndale Gang to put the pieces together on the whereabouts of the Ark of Covenant. Professor Hutchison told the Lawndale Gang that he will pick up all the expenses including travel, meals, and accommodations for this trip for a week to do this job.

So, the Lawndale Gang gathered up their things and left for Israel and when they landed in Israel the Lawndale Gang who is from Philadelphia noticed a big difference in the quality of the air. The air in Israel feels significantly hotter, drier, especially inland, and sunnier than in Philadelphia, due to its Mediterranean desert climate. Also, the Philadelphia has more humidity. That meant some adjusting was necessary.

Once the Lawndale Gang had settled in, they huddled and came to the conclusion, through research, that they would need a map of the ancient Israel and surrounding countries, which would depict the travels of the Ark in the major cities and trade routes. When they Googled this kind of map, they learned that it is called a historical atlas. Next they proceeded to the nearest book store and purchased a historical geographical map of Israel When they got back to their hotel, they spread out the map out on a table in one of the gang members' hotel room, took a marker and started to mark from the beginning of the origins of the Ark of the Covenant to the last documented whereabouts of the Ark.

One of the descriptions on the origin trail was the capture of the Ark by the Philistines, so the Lawndale Gang figured the best place to start was the Corinne Mamane Museum of Philistine Culture and talk to someone there, to see if we can unearth some clues. So, we got into our two rental cars and headed to the museum.

As we traveled to the museum, a housekeeper has entered the room where the Lawndale Gang had the historical map with their notes. It didn't take long for her to figure out that this group was trying to locate the Ark of the Covenant and she knew people that would pay her good money for this.

When the we arrived at the Philistine museum and finished a tour, we started to ask the curator questions about his thoughts on the last whereabouts of the Ark of the Covenant and surprisingly he gave us his opinion of three possible locations, which were:
1. Hidden beneath the Temple Mount in Jordan.
2. A cave on Mount Nebo in Jordan.
3. Babylon, as mentioned in the book of Jeremiah.

We thanked the curator very much for his knowledge and went to our cars and preceded to go back to our hotel. While driving back to the hotel, we noticed a car following us and suddenly the driver speed up in front of the boy's car and brought their car parallel along side the girls car with both cars taking up both lanes. The car with malevolent driver tried to run the girls off the road, in attempt to intimidate us. The boys watched in horror, as the girls tried to keep their car on the road. Suddenly the girls' car lost control and went off the road, so the boys pulled over and observed the girls car suspended on a cliff beneath the road, which was unstable. The girls panicked, since their every move made the cliff less stable

The boys arrived and they were yelling to the girls to be calm and only move if have to. Just then, one of the boys realized that they had a car kit in the vehicle with a screwdriver and thought of the idea of removing the roof rack off the top of the car and using it, to help hoist the girls off the unstable cliff, which is right below the road.

So, the boys unscrewed the roof racks and told the girls to exit one by one out of the car, but each movement caused the unstable cliff to crumble, little by little, as the each girl grabbed hold of the roof rack, while the boys hoisted them one by one to safety until all the girls were safe. They shared a group hug afterwards, but the bigger question was who and why was someone trying to run the girls off the road?

We arrived at our hotel with much discussion ahead of us as we looked at our historic map, with the new clues from the Philistine museum. We had to deduce where the Israelites would place the Ark and after careful discussion the we came to the conclusion that the highest probability is that King Solomon anticipated the Temple's destruction and prepared secret underground tunnels beneath the Temple Mount to hide the Ark from the invading Babylonians.

The next question is, who is after us? As they asked this question, there was a knock on the door. When someone from the Lawndale Gang answered the door, on the other side were three man with guns and they walked into the room demanding all the information we had relating to the Ark of Covenant. One of the girls said, "I have all the information you need in my pocketbook." While she said that, she winked to the other girls who understood what she meant. As she slowly went into her pocketbook, the girls knew what to do and as the reached they all grabbed their mace spray containers. The one girl who spoke to the men grabbed her mace spray container and said, "Here are your notes" and all the girls sprayed mace into the face of these men, which caused incredible pain and stinging in their eyes.

This allowed the boys to disarm the men, tied them up and once bound, the one boy said, "We want some answers on why you are pursuing us."

"We are both after the same thing in the Ark of the Covenant," said one of the men.

"There are other antiquities that may be more worthwhile for you, like Solomons Gold," said the boy. "Just put the pieces together from the Internet and follow your best guidance, but leave us alone since we work for a wealthy billionaire who has near limitless resources with crime fighting connections at his disposal and we'll be happy to give him all your names." The criminals agreed, and the Lawndale Gang released them.

The Lawndale Gang moved onto the next order of business, which was entering the Temple Mount that King Solomon built with its tunnels. One of the boys recommended that we sign in for a tour and check out the tunnels, but the girls have been exploring the Internet and found a metal detector that is eight inches long that could be concealed when we sign in for the tour. So, we proceeded to the Temple Mount and signed in but there was a metal detector at the entrance. When we walked through the threshold, the metal detector went off and the member with the metal detector scanner told the security guard that he had his knee replaced due to a bad football injury and that's why the metal detector was going off. Everyone was allowed to proceed afterwards.

So, we entered the tunnels with our metal detector scanner, scanning the walls and wondering where the ancient Israelites hid the Ark and waiting for the metal detector to go off because the Ark was reported to be made of gold. Suddenly, the metal detector went off, we all stopped and looked at the tunnel wall with wonder? We documented the approximate feet from the beginning of when we entered the tunnel for our investor.

The clairvoyant girl in our group said, "Wait, I'm sensing something. I'm sensing a preordained mathematical equation from beyond the wall."

Some of the Lawndale group members started to Google on their phones a parallel meaning between the Ark and math, and they found that the Ark is associated with the mathematical Golden Ratio. The Golden Ratio appears frequently in nature, art, and architecture, and its presence in the Ark's dimensions is often interpreted as evidence of a divine proportion or an underlying mathematical structure of the universe.

The Lawndale Group was in awe of the creation of the Ark of the Covenant and went back to Professor Hutchison with a job well done with all their information.

The Lawndale Gang Confronts a Drug Ring

We were driving to Prospectville, Pennsylvania to visit a member's aunt. As we were in two cars, as we usually do, on a long stretch of a two-way road the rear tire of the girls' car came off and rolled off and onto the side of the road. This caused the girls' car to lose control, veer off the side of the road, go through some brush and onto a field where the car finally stopped. The boys pulled off the side of the road to check in on the girls. The girls were okay, but everyone was mystified because they landed in a field of marijuana plants.

They were baffled as to why there were so many marijuana plants, so they decided to spread out to look around. One of the guys found a latch in the dirt, pulled on it and it was a trap door out in the middle of the field. He summoned everyone to come over and check out the trap door. There was a ladder that went down to a storage room. As they were looking into the storage room, they heard someone talking. They couldn't make out what was being said, but they heard something, so they went down the ladder. At the bottom they found a teenage girl who was tied up. A few of the guys untied her and she thanked us and warned us that we don't know what we're dealing with here. She went on to say that she accidently wondered onto the fields, was captured and tied up for several days, but she doesn't know who they are.

The Lawndale Gang huddled and concluded that who-ever tied her would be back to check on her. So, the members of the Lawndale Gang decided to look around to see if they could arm themselves. They found a few things, like a slingshot that one of the members was an expert at when he was a child, a pipe, a two by four piece of wood and a nail gun which could come in handy when defending ourselves. The problem was that we as a group weren't sure what we were up against, but it didn't look good.

It wasn't too long before the field door trap opened up and someone was coming down the ladder. Lawndale Gang hid behind the shelving, as a man approached the girl who pretended to be tied up. Little did we know that she was a black belt in Taekwondo and as he checked her roping that used to keep her tied up, she leapt, turned sideways and let her feet deliver a devasting side winder kick to the man's face, which caught him by surprise and knocked him down on his back.

The boys ran over and grabbed him, took his gun away and placed him in the chair, while they tied him up. Once tied up, they searched him and found the master plan to infiltrate the east coast with several types of illegal drugs, like marijuana, cocaine, and opioid drugs. The marijuana field is just tip of the iceberg.

So, we put our heads together and we had to gain entry to the house on the property where four or five guys are staying. We thought of the ancient Greeks where they delivered a trojan horse with soldiers hidden in it to the enemy's town, only for the enemy to be surprised by the soldiers in the trojan horse.

We decided that we should construct a 10 feet wide by 6 feet high and 4 feet deep "Trojan Crate" and once constructed, we would deliver it early in the morning, while it was still dark. The boys would hide in the crate and take on drug gang when they come out to investigate in the morning.

The boys realized that the trap door was half mile from the house where the drug smugglers were staying and felt they could build a crate with the materials they found in the shelter. The boys went to work and before they knew it, they constructed their Trojan Crate.

Next, they went through with their plan and delivered it around four o'clock in the morning. They hid patiently inside the crate with their weapons they gathered from the shelter. The drug smugglers woke up that morning and saw the crate on their front lawn. They were really baffed and a lot of talking took place among the drug smugglers, until they finally went out to investigate.

As they analyzed the crate, the boys heard footsteps outside the crate and they knew the time was now to unleash the crate's wooden wall and surprise the drug smugglers. With a crackling of urgency, the Lawndale boys unleashed the plywood wall with urgency. Their adrenaline was pumping and before you knew it, they surprised the drug smugglers, which meant a lot because they had guns and the boys had a sling shot, a nail gun, a pipe, and a 2x4 piece of wood. A big fight ensued before the smugglers were able to draw their guns, and if they could, this would be trouble for the boys. The boys pounced on them and fought over control of their guns.

While this was taking place the girls arrived at the house, grabbed the weapons that were laying on the ground, one of the weapons was the nail gun, and the girl that was tied up grabbed that and said to one of the drug smugglers "Take another move and I'll nail you alive." The four smugglers dropped their guns and as the gang was tying them up, one of the smugglers made a run for it. He ran about 20 yards before the boy, who was an expert sling shot shooter in his youth, armed the sling shot with a pebble, took aim, and released the sling shot with fury. The pebble hit the smuggler on the back of the thigh. This brought him down in pain. He was brought back and was tied up.

When the Lawndale Gang had all four of the smugglers tied up, another drug smuggler who was hiding in the house came out with a gun and held the Lawndale Gang at gun point. The girl who was a black belt in Taekwondo martial arts saw a special karate fraternity pin on his collar and she said to him, "I see you are wearing a karate fraternity pin. I'm a black belt in Taekwondo and I'll bet you I can kick your ass. So, I challenge you to a martial arts dual. So, put aside your gun and let's see if you can beat a girl."

The smuggler was not going to be spoken to that way, especially by a girl, and accepted the girl's offer. The two of them started circling each other, looking for opportunities to take advantage of each other's weaknesses.

"You think that little dance you do will save you?" The drug smuggler said.

"It's more than a dance," she replied, her voice dangerously calm.

Her black belt, a testament to years of grueling discipline, felt like a second skin. The wind picked up, rustling the dry leaves, a silent witness to the impending clash.

He lunged first, a blur of motion, a guttural roar tearing from his throat. His foot arced in a powerful roundhouse kick, aiming for her head. She ducked, the wind of his passing barely grazing her temple, the force of his strike enough to splinter bone.

"Too slow," she murmured. Her words almost lost in the wind. She spun, a whirlwind of controlled energy, her leg sweeping low. He hopped back, a surprised grunt escaping him.

He recovered quickly, his eyes narrowing, a flicker of respect, or perhaps genuine malice, in their depths. "Feisty. I like it," he said.

He came at her again, a flurry of punches, each one designed to incapacitate. She weaved, dodged, parried, her movements fluid, economical. The rhythmic thud of their feet on the hard earth, the sharp exhales of effort, punctuated the tense silence.

He landed a glancing blow to her arm, a sharp jolt of pain blossoming. She ignored it, her focus absolute. "This isn't over," he gritted out, his breath coming in ragged gasps. Sweat slicked his forehead, catching the last vestiges of light.

"No," she agreed, a faint, almost imperceptible smile touching her lips. "It's just beginning." She feigned a retreat, drawing him in, then, with explosive power, launched herself forward. A dizzying flip, her body a taut bowstring in the air. He tracked her, his guard up, but he underestimated her speed, her resolve. As her feet touched the ground, she pivoted, her hand shooting out, fingers splayed. She slammed her palm against his throat, just below his jaw, her thumb digging into the carotid artery, her other fingers pressing into the pressure points of his neck. A death grip.

His eyes widened, bulging. A strangled gurgle escaped him, his hands scrabbling uselessly at her arm. His body stiffened, then sagged, his legs giving way. She held him, her gaze unwavering, until the last flicker of life left his eyes, until his bulky form slumped to the ground, a silent heap in the gathering darkness.

The wind died down, leaving an unnatural stillness. She stood over him, her chest heaving, the scent of fear replaced by the metallic tang of victory.

Everybody stood still, absorbing the moment s since no one wanted the loss of a life, but these drug smugglers had no respect for life. The bottom line was this: It was his life or our life. We consoled the girl who put her life on the line to help us.

With the drug smugglers tied up, we looked at their computer hardware. Their network of drug connections was vast. One of the girls in our group was very proficient in information technology suggested that we upload a virus into their network that will ultimately compromise their computer and make it impossible for them to do business.

She uploaded the virus and the gang called the police to give a synopsis on the situation and left the drug smugglers tied up for when the police arrived. The Lawndale Gang drove down the gravel road that led out to the main road as the sun was coming up. For each day is a new day of opportunity in the lives of the Lawndale Gang.

A New Frontier

While walking in Tookany park in Cheltenham, Pennsylvania, one of the members of the Lawndale Gang had their dog and he went off the beaten path, as dogs like to wander. The dog found something in the foliage and he kept pointing to it and barking at it.

The Lawndale Gang went over to investigate. They had to clear a lot of sticks and leaves out of the way, since it was off the beaten path. As they cleared away foliage they started to realize there was something significant beneath the surface, so they kept digging.

To our astonishment, they found a spacecraft that must crashed years ago. We heard of the stories of alien sightings in the area, and how aliens may have been involved throughout our history. Now here it is, an actual spacecraft So, we looked around the ship and there was enough seating for all of us.

We looked at the navigation system and it looked like there was pre-set coordinates assigned to the craft. We wondered if the navigation system was assigned to the aliens' home planet. We thought long and hard about this and discussed on whether we should attempt to let this spacecraft lead us to its home planet or not. We considered the pros and cons of our greatest explorers like Ameilia Earhart, Neil Armstrong, and Leif Erikson. They all had something in common, they like breaking barriers, challenging the status quo, and discovering new frontiers.

We found this encouraging as we sat on the threshold of opportunity and decided that we were not going to let this opportunity pass us by. We buckled our seatbelts for an adventure of a lifetime and hit the ignition. We let the coordinates take us on this adventure. We lifted off as the ship's navigation systems knew exactly what to do, and soon enough we were traveling through space at an unbelievable speed, with the celestial body of stars that were so breathtaking to witness. After a while, we entered a worm hole where time and space have their own calibrations. As we went through the hole, we witnessed what Earth looked like at the beginning of time when it was known for its volcanic gases, as well as sulfur and carbon dioxide emissions.

The next thing we knew we were out of the worm hole heading for another planet and the ship was trying to land us safely. Unfortunately, we crashed in dense rain forest. Many of us were banged up pretty good from the crash, with lots of bumps, sprains, and bruises. We were still buckled in and trying to recover from the crash, when an older man approached us with a brown hooded cloak, a cream-colored tunic and leather boots. He helped us, took us back to his cave where he lived took care of us, until we felt better.

While we were there, he showed us ancient scrolls he found in this cave 25 years ago that were full of wisdom and spirituality. He gave us lessons on thought provoking wisdom that we never considered, such as God's natural world is all around us, the cosmos, atoms, photons, trees, oceans, creeks, rocks, crystals, and let's not forget the oxygen we breathe.

The truth has its own set of laws and math, which can't be suppressed. Over time, the truth always seems to come to the surface because of its own values from above. To help facilitate bringing things into fruition, prayer is a petition to God or whomever you worship, for action tended to activate your request through worship will bring things into materialization. Also, to help bring things into fruition, you need to weigh the changes you need to make in order to receive more abundant graces from God.

And so, the lessons went on for six months under this wise hermit's guidance. During this process, we learned to live off the land, we slowly regained our health and were ready to leave the rain forest. We hiked for many miles until we found a city. Once we found urban life beyond the rain forest, we walked around in this new world, marveling at the difference between Earth and this new planet, then we heard screams for help.

We ran to where the screams were coming from and to our astonishment they led us to a two-story building with flames coming from the windows upstairs. A mother was hanging out of the one remaining window upstairs calling for help because she and her child were trapped upstairs. The Lawndale Gang went into action. We saw some clothing drying on a clothesline in the backyard, so we covered ourselves with as much clothes as possible, took a garden hose and showered each other with water, until all of us were soaked. All of us entered the house and we had to run through some flames to get upstairs. We reached the mother and child as the flames intensified, so one of the girls wrapped up the child under her wet clothing. We also brought some extra wet clothing for the mother, and had to make mad dash to leave the house, as the flames started to surround us.

By the time we left the house, there were about 30 people who had gathered outside the house, along with some fire trucks. The fire chief wanted to know who we were and where we came from, since we shared with him the only identification we had on us, which was from Earth. That only brought more questions because he never heard of Earth. The fire chief contacted his superiors and the Lawndale Gang was sequestered for further questioning.

The police captain arrived and looked at the identifications of the Lawndale Gang's origin. The captain was baffled and never heard of their city country, or planet. So, the Lawndale Gang were ushered off to police headquarters for further questioning. Once the Lawndale Gang arrived, the captain started to think that the Lawndale Gang were extraterrestrials. A higher governmental authority was brought in, known as G.F.T.P., which stood for Government For The People agency and they started to question the Lawndale Gang.

An agent from GFTP asked, "Where did you kids come from?"

"We come from Philadelphia, Pennsylvania in the United States of America," said a girl member of the Lawndale Gang.

"Where is that?" the GFTP agent asked.

"We come from a planet called Earth, and we found one of your ships in a park. It must have been there for a while. The coordinates were pre-set and since we are explorers of knowledge, we got in and the ship took us here. We crashed in the rain forest and lived off the land for six months while living in a cave," said a boy member of the Lawndale Gang.

"Where did this ship crash?" asked the GFTP agent.

"Out beyond the river where the cliffs are steep and there are many large birds nesting on the cliffs," said another girl member of the Lawndale Gang.

You mean you crashed beyond the great peninsula," said the GFTP agent. "That's impossible! No man has been out there, survived and walked out of the rain forest."

"We were pretty banged up from our crash and we had to heal up," said another boy member of the Lawndale Gang. "An old wise man helped us and led us back to his cave. There he nurtured us, gave us shelter and provided us with wisdom that he found from ancient scrolls when he first inhabited the cave. He helped us get our strength back to walk out of the rain forest, but we believe all things happen for a reason. Let us explain, when your intentions are good it sets in motion the wheels and mechanics that if you believe in the impossible and if you combine with good intentions, then anything is possible for you".

"Where did you learn that?" the GFTP agent asked.

We found spiritual ancient scrolls in one of the caves out beyond the peninsula," said a girl member of the Lawndale Gang. "We think we can give you a general idea where it is, if you provide us with a map.

"What else did you learn?" asked the GFTP agent.

"If we want to get the most out of life, then we must fulfill it without fear," said a boy member of the Lawndale Gang. "Fear inhibits us and stunts our growth. Overcoming fear allows us to grow and reach our full potential. It is significant to realize that as we read more positive content, this helps us challenge our fears and expand our mind. We can then think and wonder with boundless imagination. This helps us create ideas that can only be a result of being free of fear."

"This is so important when you want to unleash the power of your mind," added a girl member of the Lawndale Gang "When you release the power of your mind, there is no relevance between achieving perception of the significance and awareness of the size and scope of the material world when it comes to your life. The scope of the material world is immeasurable in relation to what you can achieve when you believe."

"Nothing is impossible for you," added another boy member of the Lawndale Gang. "If a person perishes under a tree and part of his matter decomposes into the soil, does that person then become part of that tree? The answer is yes, because we're all a part of the same fabric of the universe, which is atoms, protons, electrons, and neutrons. And it becomes the essence of that tree."

"This old man that helped you? We wonder if it could be Kurt Wagner who went into the rain forest about 25 years ago and he didn't return," said the GFTP agent. "We sent a search party for him, but no one found his body. I wonder if it could be him? Nevertheless, this ancient scroll might have been left by the indigenous tribes that lived in that area for thousands of years and we're not too sure what happened to them. We have to find these ancient scrolls and possibly Kurt Wagner for better teachings for our people. In the meantime, you are our guest, but please don't leave the facility until we straighten this whole thing out."

Several days went by, and with the guidance from the Lawndale Gang, the search team found the ancient scrolls and identified the wise old man, as Kurt Wagner. They were both brought back to GFTP headquarters, where there was a reunion between Kurt and the Lawndale Gang.

The GFTP agents were excited for the new teachings and Kurt Wagner was appointed as Minister of Wisdom for their nation. The GFTP wanted to hold a special celebration in honor of the Lawndale Gang and Kurt Wagner. The doors opened and the Lawndale Gang never thought in their wildest dreams that they would be honored in this way. They came down the center path, which separated all the dignitaries and the staffing on the right and left, and they approached the stage for what the people of this planet call the, Medal of Legacy. The Lawndale Gang stood so proudly with their medals and faced everyone who thanked them for a job well done. Next, plans were made for a spacecraft to return the Lawndale Gang back to Earth.

Bonnie and Clyde

By now, the Lawndale Gang has become a well-known crime solving team, and the Philadelphia Correction Facility asked them to give a motivational speech to troubled teenagers. Since the Lawndale Gang just moved beyond the teenage years, into young adulthood. the officials at the correction facility thought they would be a good example for troubled teenagers.

So, the Lawndale Gang was ushered into a gym that had bleachers, and the troubled teens came in and sat down in the chairs in the gym. The Lawndale Gang were on the bleachers in order to be elevated when they spoke.

"Whatever circumstances that caused you to be placed here are not bigger than the solution to right yourself," said a boy member of the Lawndale Gang "We don't care what the circumstances you are in, because nothing is impossible to you when you put your mind to it."

"It all starts with the mind, because you have to get the mind right, and you do that with contemplation, which is deep and focused thought," said a girl member of the Lawndale Gang. "From the mind, everything grows that is natural, as long as your intentions are good. The universe will unravel a natural law, provided your intentions are good. It's the natural progression of the universe."

"The thing is you have to put the time in and apply yourself," said another boy member of the Lawndale Gang . "It's a collective effort that will unshackle your mind and unleash your hidden power because the universe, as we know, is continuously expanding. The potential for growth is boundless, like our universe, and we are a microcosm of the universe, so our potential is unlimited, as long as we believe. We wish you the best of luck in your journey, and remember your biggest ally comes from above. So please, don't forget to pray."

There was an inmate there that was reformed and due to his good behavior, he was asked to participate in this session. He was also put on the security detail during this session between the Lawndale Gang and the troubled teenagers. After the session concluded, he approached the Lawndale Gang and told them in private of a bank robbery he was involved 20 years ago. The money was located at the base of a tree on at a colonial mansion located in Wrightstown, Pennsylvania, which was the former residence of the governor.

"It would be easy to find if you look at the back door and look straight into the yard," the inmate said. "You'll see a large oak tree, and that's where I buried my loot from my heist, which I'm not proud of. Anyway, I would like you to dig it up and donate it to

Shriners Hospital for Children, because my brother's daughter was diagnosed with scoliosis. Shriners Hospital attended to my niece's medical needs, and fitted her with a special back brace. I buried $25,000 from the heist and along with the money, is a document that tells the truth about the heroism involved with capturing Bonnie and Clyde."

"Most people don't know the truth about the capture of Bonnie and Clyde," the inmate went on to say. "I would like you kids to donate the money and help me spread the word about the truth of the events that led to the capture of Bonnie and Clyde."

The Lawndale Gang assured him they would do all they could to help him, and then the Lawndale Gang wished him well on as he works towards his release.

After leaving the correctional facility, the Lawndale Gang looked up maps surrounding the governor's mansion in Wrightstown, and learned that there is a parking lot separating the wooded area between the backyard and the governor's mansion. This would be good access for the Lawndale Gang to park and to gain entry undetected to the wooded area where the oak tree is, and to both dig up the money and the information on Bonnie and Clyde.

Once there, the Lawndale Gang succeeded in digging up the canister containing the money and documents about the true events that led to Bonnie and Clyde's capture.

Texas governor, Miriam Ferguson in 1934 hired a retired Texas Ranger, named Frank Hammer to find

Bonnie and Clyde. Governor Ferguson told Hammer to"Stop Bonnie and Clyde, by any means necessary." Bonnie and Clyde were involved in a two-year crime spree, from 1932 -1934, which resulted in the deaths of 12 people, including 9 law enforcement officers. Frank Hammer led a special investigation that brought Bonnie and Clyde to justice by studying their movement patterns across state lines. After a 100-day pursuit, Hammer and his team ambushed and killed the couple in Louisiana on May 23, 1934.

The Lawndale Gang were inspired by the true story behind the bravery and ability of Frank Hammer, who outsmarted Bonnie and Clyde. They also wanted to keep their promise to the inmate at the correctional facility. So they approached a friend who was into social media and email marketing and he took the typed document that the Lawndale Gang created about the work of Texas Ranger Frank Hammer. and the friend sent it out to mass email distribution list of 100,000 email addresses. The Lawndale Gang thought this was a good start to spread the good news about the capture of Bonnie and Clyde.

The next order of business was to donate the $25,000 that was stolen 25 years ago. The Lawndale Gang drove to Shriners Hospital in Philadelphia. They walked in the front door and told the receptionist they would like to donate $25,000 dollars. The story they told the receptionist was that this money was saved for years by one of the member's grandmother. She just passed away and they would like to make a donation on her behalf.

This story is dedicated to all law enforcement for their dedication and the tireless hours they work for protecting their communities.

Samurai Warrior Code

The Lawndale Gang thought they could use some exposure to culture and they decided to visit the Great Wall of China. The Great Wall is 2,700 years old and was built by different dynasties.

The Lawndale Gang arrives in China and is taking part in a tour of the Great Wall of China. Along the way, the Lawndale Gang learns that there are 220 hidden doors in the Great Wall of China, and these secret passages were designed for soldiers to conduct surprise attacks, communicate, and manage trade without compromising the wall's defense integrity. Therefore, the Lawndale Gang thought it would be fascinating educational experience to enter through one of these hidden doors.

So that's what they did, and they entered a passage in the Ming Dynasty section, when no one was looking. The passages were narrow and very old looking. It felt as if they were going through history because these hidden passages were over 2,000 years old. They stumbled onto a bunch of bones that were in an old fire pit. This baffled the Lawndale Gang, so some members pulled out their smartphones and learned that these bones represented an old Chinese mysticism called oracle bones. These bones were used to call upon the heavens and ask for divine intervention on the practitioner's behalf.

So, the members of the Lawndale Gang are looking at the bones, and all of a sudden, a door opens up before them. It looks like a portal and the Lawndale Gang had to make a quick decision on what to do, since they didn't know how long the doorway was going to stay opened. So, the Lawndale Gang decided quickly to jump through the portal door, since they believed that everything happens for a reason.

After jumping through the door, they ended up in beautiful rolling hills and valleys in Japan. The Lawndale Gang was astounded as to where they were, but it wasn't too long before they heard horses galloping towards them. As the horses came closer, they could see that the men wore armor layered for battle and when they stopped, the girls were concerned, since the men were wearing menacing attire.

The men dismounted and said, "We are the culture of the samurai, who are you?" As the one samurai said this, another walked over to one of our girls, took off his glove and moved his index finger down her cheek. She turned away from him in disgust.

One of our toughest guys from our group didn't like that gesture and ran over and shoved him to the ground, shocking the other 12 Samurai on horses, including the Shogun, who was a king-like figure.
The samurai that was shoved, got up and felt he was not shown proper respect. He asked the Shogun to

regain his respect by fighting to the death to the person who shoved him down. The Shogun gave his nod of approval. The other samurai gave a sword and a shield to the person who shoved the samurai to the ground and the two squared off for a fight to the death.

"You believe this street rat can truly challenge a warrior of the Shogun?" the Shogun, known as Lord Hiroshi, asked.

He fights with a hunger, my Lord," an attendant murmured, adjusting his gaze to our friend and added: "Unorthodox, but effective."

The Samurai moved first, a blur of disciplined grace. His sword sang as it cleaved the air, aiming for our friend's collarbone. However, the collarbone didn't meet the blade, as he ducked, shield angled high, deflecting the attack with a jarring thud. The Samurai's eyes, cold and focused, narrowed.

"Is that all you offer?" the Samurai's voice, a low growl, barely carried on the wind. "A dodge and a block?"

Our friend slips a feral grin and said, "Plenty more where that came from, fancy boy." His counter was unexpected. Instead of a classic parry, he lunged low, sweeping his shield not to block, but to trip. The Samurai, caught off balance, stumbled, his foot sliding on the loose earth. He recovered instantly, but the momentary disruption was enough. Our friend's broadsword, heavy and blunt, slammed against the Samurai's shield, the impact rattling the warrior's arm.

Lord Hiroshi leaned forward, a flicker of interest in his usually impassive eyes. "He uses his shield as a weapon, not just defense," he said.

The Samurai, regaining his posture, advanced with renewed ferocity. His attacks became a whirlwind, each strike precise, intended to find a weakness in our friends less refined stance. Our friend met them, not with textbook blocks, but with jarring, almost clumsy deflections, turning the Samurai's force against him, guiding the blows away, never truly engaging blade to blade in a sustained parry. He preferred to use his shield to batter and create openings, a street brawler's grim improvisation. He danced, he weaved, he twisted, his movements a chaotic symphony against the Samurai's rigid ballet.

"You fight like a cornered beast!" the Samurai bellowed, his breath coming in short, sharp bursts. His armor, once pristine, now bore scuff marks from our friends relentless, unconventional assaults.

Our friend chuckled, a harsh, dry sound. "And you fight like a book," he said. "Predictable."

He lunged, drawing the Samurai's guard high, then dropped, sweeping his sword in a wide, horizontal arc. The Samurai jumped, a feat of agility, but the movement left his side exposed. Our friend didn't miss the chance. His shield, edge-first, slammed into the Samurai's ribs. A grunt of pain escaped the warrior; his breath momentarily knocked from his lungs. The Samurai staggered back, clutching his side. His shield clattered to the ground, his posture broken. Lord Hiroshi rose from his seat, his voice cutting through the tense air, echoing across the silent hills. "Enough!"

Both combatants froze, their chests heaving. The Samurai, wincing, looked towards his Lord, then at our friend, a new, grudging respect dawning in his eyes. Our friend, still panting, lowered his sword, his gaze fixed on the Shogun.

"This fight is over," Lord Hiroshi declared, his voice firm, yet tinged with a new tone. "You have gained my respect, street fighter. You have shown us a different kind of strength and skill. One I did not know existed." He looked at our friend, and with a slow nod said, "Serve me. Your unorthodox methods may prove invaluable."

The Shogun continued, "I welcome you all back to my village, and you will learn our culture and our ways" As the Lawndale Gang walked back to the village, they all agreed to meet and keep in touch, as they learn the customs of the Samurai culture.

The boy's kept themselves busy with learning archery, practicing swordsmanship and maintaining weapons. The girls were being trained in martial arts because, in the tradition of the Samurai, it was important to defend the household while the men were away during sieges. In the meantime, the Lawndale Gang met late at night, by the stable to collect their thoughts and commune with each other, as they had done throughout their years together.

On this night, they had heard of a palm reader coming to the village to do her divination, which involved fortune-telling and analyzing hand lines for a person's well-being. When the palm reader came, she took her time and studied each of the Lawndale Gang's palms.

The palm reader was analyzing them with great detail, and she gave her collective analysis of the group.

"Your group is on a level of consciousness that your true self is not limited to the physical body," said the palm reader. "This perspective suggests that you are a temporary visitor in this physical reality, often described as a astral traveler. With the destiny that is unclear at this time."

We walked away wondering what might this destiny could be? But one thing we thought was clear, whatever it was, we have to be patient and let time and the physical world reveal this destiny to us when the time was right.

Therefore, we continued our daily practices of learning the samurai culture until one day we entered a chamber that we were told was off limits. Our curiosity got the best of us, so we entered the chamber and started to look around. We found an ancient chest. We opened it and we found a scroll that read, "From far away a group emerges that stirs the imagination. They believed in themselves and provided hope since their convictions run deep and strengthens our culture with vision and hope for a new tomorrow."

As the Lawndale Gang read this scroll, they couldn't help but think that this scroll was talking about them. Taking this scroll and its message, and combining it with what the palm reader was predicting for the Lawndale Gang, they thought that a great honor was going to be given to them to carry out. Still, they needed to be patient and wait for this opportunity and destiny to reveal itself.

Weeks go by and the Lawndale Gang is still meeting each night at the horse stables and they are still doing daily activities. They soon hear the word of a bloody showdown with a rival samurai clan over regional dominance to become the Shogun in that area.

The Lawndale Gang thought about what this meant. They realized that this was their moment and destiny that the palm reader and scroll was talking about . They had to reach within themselves to get their thoughts together, in order to approach the Shogun with the scroll and try to convince him that they are here for a purpose and their destiny is to avoid unnecessary bloodshed.

So, the Lawndale Gang made an appointment with the Shogun. When they appeared before him, they said, "Master, we heard of the upcoming battle with the rival samurai clan. We heard it may cause a lot of bloodshed and we ask you to let peace prevail because we feel every effort of peace and understanding should be made before bloodshed."

Who are you to weigh in on such a matter?" asked the Shogun.

"If it means anything to you," said one boy member of the Lawndale Gang. "We found this ancient scroll in one of your chests in the forbidden room, which we humbly apologize for entering. Nevertheless, we would like to share it with you."

The Shogun read the scroll. When finished he says: "This scroll was written several hundred years ago.

It was based on a prediction by a fortune teller and was packed away. I totally forgot about it. Still, what do you propose?"

"We would like to meet with the rival clan as ambassadors of your Samurai clan to help negotiate a peace deal where everyone is happy," said a girl member of the Lawndale Gang. "It would be our honor to represent you."

The Shogun gives his nod of approval and wonders to himself, *Who are these kids and where did they come from?*

The Lawndale Gang arrives at the rival Samurai's village and they are escorted before the Shogun of that clan.

"Greetings exalted one," said a boy member of the Lawndale Gang. "We seek to meet with you, share ideas and explore your great wisdom on a deal that will benefit you and the samurai clan we represent, in order to avoid bloodshed between both of you. We are travelers of both time and space, and we feel were placed here for a reason and now our calling has brought us before you to help us fulfill our destiny, as we the Lawndale Gang, pass on the ancient scroll, which is dated and signed by a legendary fortune teller."

"I have heard of these wives' tales that have been passed down through many generations and this is very fascinating to me," said the rival samurai "I'll listen to what you have to say."

"Where we come from, the true power of a warrior is in his heart," said a girl member of the Lawndale Gang. "What we have learned over the centuries is that there are many intangibles of the heart. Yes, one is bravery and the other one is seeking peace and understanding before conflict. Both elements work together in unison. The heart is not singular. It is multifaceted in its function. We are asking you to seek peace before conflict, Exalted One."

"You talk of truths that are new to me," said the rival Samurai. "I will allow you to meet the other Shogun with a delegation from me and we'll do all the arranging, you are dismissed."

It took the Lawndale Gang all day to travel by foot to meet the other Shogun, and once before the other Shogun, who knew that they came to represent the other clan, he was not friendly to them and said bluntly, "What do you want?"

"Does a man who seeks knowledge ever get thirsty?" asked a girl member of the Lawndale Gang.

"You seem to draw from a wisdom that is beyond our limits that we call an old soul," said the other Shogun. "I will hear your plea."

Your perception of power is wrapped up in conquering and boundaries and we are here to let you know of a greater power where you can have the best of both worlds, without all the bloodshed," said a boy member of the Lawndale Gang. "Because a true warrior needs control, discipline and focus. These principles come from the mind, because when you combine the Samurai warrior code with discipline, you are removing impulse and replacing it with focus. We feel this will make your clan stronger. So, we're asking to apply focus and discipline to stop this brutal, unnecessary bloodshed. You can both honor the Samurai code at a higher level, which we call real power."

"You talk of a power I think we should learn," said the other Shogun. "Tell your Shogun I accept your terms, and perhaps someday we'll sit across from each other discussing our virtues."

The Lawndale Gang returned to their hometown, and shared the good news with their Shogun that the brutal bloodshed was averted. The other Shogun extended his appreciation by offering hopeful dialogue between the two clans in the future.

"Job well done. The boys will be decorated with a special shield from me in gratitude," said the Shogun. "The girls will receive a special martial arts belt with our clan's motto on it, for all to see how appreciative I am of your efforts."

That night when the Lawndale Gang met at the horse stable they were feeling pretty good about their accomplishment. Unbeknown to them, the universe, who set them on this path to begin with, also was aware of their accomplishments. While the Lawndale gang was celebrating, the same portal door appeared before, was opening up again in the middle of the night next to the horse stable. The Lawndale Gang knew what this meant. Since the universe is aware of all things that need to be done with its perfect timing. The Lawndale Gang jumped through the portal door, ending up at Magee and Oakley, where it all began.

Music Evokes Emotion

The Lawndale Gang was invited to a wedding reception. When we got there, we asked the maître d if he wouldn't mind letting us sit at a banquet table, so all 15 of us could sit together. The DJ did a good job mixing up the cocktail music and the dinner music. In the mix, were dance and slow songs to accommodate all the ages.

As the reception was proceeding throughout the night, we were talking amongst ourselves about how music was so powerful that it evoked deep emotions out of people. We witnessed old people sentimentally dancing with each other as they listened to the music and the saw the embraces between them from long enduring marriages. We saw new couples looking deep into each other's eyes as a new romance lifted their spirits. We watched how people danced to two different tempos as the dance music played.

One of our members was going to Community College of Philadelphia, and that person was taking a course called, Introduction to Research, which was a class on how to do a research paper and he thought that how music evokes emotion would be a great subject for a research paper.

So, as the night was winding down, we heard there was a music professor in attendance at the reception. So, we approached him and asked, "Professor, what was the origin of music?"

"That's a good question," said the professor. "In actuality the first musical instruments were ivory and bone flutes discovered in German cave, dating back 40,000."

Incidentally, the week before one of the girls won a decent sum of money from a scratch off lottery ticket. So, the Lawndale Gang thought it would be a great idea to take a trip to southern Germany to see the caves where the origin of music occurred. They felt this would be a great help for their friend's research paper, and to some sightseeing for the group, as well.

We booked the next plane to southern Germany and went on a tour of the Hollow Rock Cave, which yielded the world's oldest instrument. This instrument was a bird bone flute dating back approximately 40,000 years. A bird bone flute was crafted from the hollow wing bones of birds, such as waterfowl or raptors.

We decided to explore the cave on our own and separated from the tour group, and when deeper into the cave. Out of the corner of our eyes, we saw something that looked like a walking stick, which was covered by rocks in the corner of the cave. We walked over and removed the rocks carefully and to our surprise we found a very old walking stick. At the top of the walking stick was a ruby. We studied the walking stick and it looked like it had a deliberate design.

As the tour guide and the visitors left to cave, we stayed behind to investigate some more. As the sun went down, a stream of light came in through the back of the cave, almost like a laser. As we watched this stream of light coming through the back of the cave and one of the boys got the idea to put the staff with the ruby in the direct stream of light so that the light would go through the ruby. Once he did that the most astonishing thing happened. We saw a hologram of Jesus giving instructions to the people that were living approximately 40,000 years ago. We kept watching this miracle that God allowed this message from the future to be relayed to these early people for guidance.

When Jesus was finished speaking, it transitioned to a hologram of the Buddha. We then watched the Buddha give instructions to people living 40,000 years ago. When the Buddha was finished, the last hologram was Shiva of the Hindus and he giving instructions to these early humans for guidance, as well as for hope and survival.

We stood there and marveled at what this meant. Early humans received guidance and instructions from above from our greatest Earthly spiritual teachers. We contemplated among ourselves what to do with this information? Should we tell the authorities? If we tell the authorities, would they want to come in and investigate what we found was a miracle from above to provide hope to our early humans? Do we want investigative teams to dissect every inch of this cave? We came to the conclusion that the best thing to do is to walk out of this cave and not mention anything to anyone, so as not to disturb the miraculous details of what we discovered.

Our friend has gathered a wealth of information for his research paper. As we were on our plane ride home, we thought about how God works his miracles through so many details of orchestration that are unknown to us, because it's impossible for us to know the infinite mind of God.

The Time Is Now

Noah Buergi, the fourth-generation descendant of the Swiss clockmaker Jost Buergi contacted the Lawndale Gang, by way of their website and asked them if he would like to meet them. Noah agreed to meet the Lawndale Gang at their fort to discuss important information.

So, they met at the fort and Noah starts off by giving a history of timekeeping. Around 3500 BC, Egyptians used sundials to measure time. Egyptians and Persians used water clocks for nighttime timekeeping, measuring the flow of water. China and other cultures used time candles and fire clocks for the passage of time. The ancient Sumerians and Babylonians devised a system of dividing hours into 60 minutes and minutes into 60 seconds. Mechanical clocks appeared in Europe during the 14th century. Pendulum Clocks were invented in the 1600s, increasing accuracy significantly. In the 18th century, the Swiss transformed clock-making from a craft into a precise, high-volume industry by pioneering a production system that specialized in pocket watches. This lasted until the early 20th century, when wristwatches gained popularity.

"I have invented a watch that will revolutionize the watch industry by using internal power and never requiring a battery," said Buergi "Before I launch my invention, marketing experts always advise the importance of knowing your competition inside and out, in order to position your platforms for success."

He continued, "This is where you guys come in. Seiko released the world's first commercially available quartz wristwatch on Christmas Day, December 25, 1969, in Tokyo. This revolutionized the industry, since it achieved 100 times the accuracy of mechanical watches. Your job, if you decide to take it, is to learn Seiko's technology on how the quartz watch works, which is top secret. I'm not going to use this information against them, but it will help me position my brand for its launch and identify a better platform for my marketing."

The Lawndale Gang agreed to take on this assignment and began working to determine the best way to proceed. They devised a plan to go to the Seiko contact page and say that they are doing a college project on the progression of timekeeping and they are watch inventors, as well. They would like to know if Seiko would share their information on the quartz watch.

The desk person at Seiko Watches, whose name was Albert, was an inventor himself and he wanted to help the Lawndale Gang. They arranged to meet Albert at the fort, along with Noah. When they all met with Albert, that's when Noah stepped forward and explained his invention, which was a self-propelled wristwatch which will never need a battery. It would use a kinetic rotor to store energy in a main spring, using biokinetic resonation. This technology receives micro-vibrations pulses from body heat generated through skin movement. This produces a constant, limitless low-voltage charge, giving the consumer the ability to power a wristwatch for a lifetime.

Noah asked Albert whether he knew the secrets of Seiko's quartz watch. Albert told him the details and explained how Seiko's quartz watch worked. A Seiko quartz watch functions by using a battery to send electricity through a quartz crystal, causing it to vibrate at a precise frequency. With an integrated circuit which counts the vibrations and converts them into a certain amount of electric pulses per second, this drives the motor to move the hands on the watch.

Noah thanked Albert and told him he will not use this information against Seiko, but it will help him understand how to better position his own new watch when he launches it. Albert asked if he could be a contributor in his new invention, Noah said yes, and a new alliance was born.

From the time when humans first realized they could use bones from the beast they hunted to settle tribal territory disputes with other clans to the invention of the wheel, the invention of language, the invention of aviation, the invention of the telephone, humans has always been called to climb the highest pinnacle in innovation. For using our time to advance our knowledge will always be our greatest investment.

Deborah Sampson

The Lawndale Gang wanted to take a road trip to tour some historic locomotive trains at a railroad museum in Stroudsburg, Pennsylvania, which was an hour and a half drive from Philadelphia. While there they decided to check out the iconic 1875 Tahoe locomotive. They were able to get a tour of this magnificent locomotive of the past and while touring the train, the tour guide was distracted. Some of the members of the Lawndale Gang were a little curious and were looking around this fantastic locomotive.

After looking around this train they decided to sit down for a little while at a very old dining room table. One of the dining room chair legs was wobbly, so one of the boys had a Swiss Army Knife with all kinds of tightening tools. He turned the chair upside down to tighten the leg, which he did. When he turned the chair upside down, he found a package taped to the bottom of the chair.

The Lawndale Gang opened the package only to find instructions that this locomotive was specially designed by Dr. Furgeson, who as a physicist from the 18th century. It said that there is a special panel in the engineering room that will help you generate a traversable wormhole, which is a shortcut through time and space. Part of the engine is designed to generate an intense magnetic field and a singularity that opens the portal, allowing the locomotive train to connect across space and time without moving through conventional space. In other words, we could move to other dimensions without the train moving at all.

The instructions went on to say that this transversal wormhole will only last 12 hours, before it returns you to your original reality. So, we huddled up together and thought that since we have the instructions on how to transport ourselves through time and space without physically moving the train, we agreed that this could be the journey of a lifetime.

We maneuvered ourselves to the front of the train where the engineering room was and we had to look for that special panel. The panel was locked. Luckily, one of our members was skilled at lock picking and was able to pick the lock with one of the girls' hairpins.

Once the panel was opened, we saw devices that helped compute traversable, time-bending wormholes, like an advanced multi-dimensional interface meter, a gravitational and quantum data meter, and the spatial curvature reader with a lever and a power button. We all strapped ourselves in and pushed the power button and pulled the lever down. Th next thing we knew we were on the railroad tracks in a beautiful open valley area and the train came to a stop. We got off the train and started to walk down a dirt road until we came upon a farm house where the owner of the farm house was attending his livestock and our presence surprised him.

The farmer's name was Fred. He welcomed us in his barn and we all sat down on benches to chat.

"Where are you kids from?" he asked us.

"We're from Philadelphia Fred," said a girl member of the Lawndale Gang

"You're in the farmlands of Massachusetts," said Fred.

"What year is it, Fred?" A boy member of the Lawndale Gang asked.

"It's 1900," said Fred.

"Oh my God, we're from the year 1980," said another girl member of the Lawndale Gang. "Please sir, you got to believe us, but we were transported through time. It's a long story, but we can't believe that our transversal wormhole machine actually worked."

"Hold on, you say you kids are from the future," said Fred. "That would explain why you are dressed differently. Of course, we have to figure out why you're here. According to my thinking, everything has a purpose. So, there's got to be a reason why you're here."

He paused, then said, "We're coming up on our annual celebration of Deborah Sampson. I wonder if that has anything to do with it? The universe has a way of correcting and bringing the truth to the surface."

Who is Deborah Samspon?" another boy member of the Lawndale Gang asked.

"Deborah Samson was a Massachusetts woman who disguised herself as a man to enlist in the Continental Army during the Revolutionary War," said Fred. "She served for 17 months in the Fourth Massachusetts Regiment, where she fought in combat, sustained wounds, and was honored for her bravery. Deborah was honorably discharged in 1783. Later, she became one of the first women to receive a full military pension. She was self-educated and worked as a teacher before enlisting."

He continued, "While fighting in Tarrytown, NY, she was shot in the thigh. To avoid detection, she removed the musket ball herself. Her secret was discovered in 1783, while she was ill with fever in Philadelphia. If what you said was true about this temporary portal you came through, I can't think of a higher cause then you kids going back to the future and helping spread the word about Deborah Sampson. She is an unsung hero in our American history. By the way, would you kids like to join me for lunch?"

"Our temporary traversable portal is only open for 12 hours, but we think we have enough time to have lunch with you," said another girl member of the Lawndale Gang.

After lunch, we strapped ourselves into our seats ten minutes before our 12-hour temporary portal in 1900 was up and the next thing we knew, we were being transported through the Milky Way. We saw an incredible dense field of stars, far more numerous and vivid than earth. Without atmospheric distortion, stars appear as sharp, steady pinpoints of intense light against a deep void within our galaxy. It was breathtaking to watch and before we know it, we were back in the railroad museum in Stroudsburg right where it all began with our knowledge of the history of Deborah Sampson, the unsung hero of the Revolutionary War. She showed bravery and courage, while disguised as man. We are going to do our part to celebrate her legacy and bring her story to the public's eye because as Fred told us, the truth has a way finding its way to the surface.

Solomon's Gold

One of the Lawndale Gang's members grandmom was in hospice and she summoned the Lawndale Gang to be by her side. As she spoke her last few words, she told the Lawndale Gang how she was engaged to a Saudi Prince when she was 20 years old and he would tell her stories that he knew where King Solomon's gold was hidden.

"The prince would tell me where it was and one day I took the time to write this down," said the grandmom. "The map is in my pocketbook which I would like to give to you. I hope you can bring closure to one of the greatest mysteries of our time."

She went on to say, "Our engagement didn't last, but I held on to the map and wasn't sure what to do with it. With your investigative skills, I'm going to put this in your good hands. Good luck and God Speed." Then member's grandmom slipped into twilight's last gleaming.

The Lawndale Gang had to do some historical fact-finding on King Solomon's gold. King Solomon amassed immense wealth, estimated by some to be roughly a billion dollars in modern value, through a combination of vast international trade networks, strategic alliances, heavy taxation, and massive tribute payments. King Solomon ruled Israel for 40 years. His reign was often termed as a golden age, since it was characterized by immense prosperity. In addition, there was the construction of the first temple in Jerusalem, and significant territorial expansion.

According to our member's grandmom's map, Solomon's gold is hidden in a chamber in the Timna Valley in southern Israel. There is a deep groundwater well in the Timna Valley, which you would need to access in order to go underground. Once there, you will find a secret passageway to a chamber where Solomon's gold is located.

The Lawndale Gang researched how many deepwater underground wells were in the Timna Valley in southern Israel, and there was only one. They realized that this information made their assignment much more easier. While the Lawndale Gang was taking their plane to Israel, they couldn't help but wonder what would it would mean if they found King Solomon's gold. Historians have speculated about the value of King Solomon's gold. They agreed that if they found King Solomon's gold, they would make a generous donation to charity, and perhaps give up crime solving in order move on in their lives and use some of the money to fuel their interests.

They land at Ben Gurion Airport, and learn about the location of this underground well. They also learned that this is no ordinary well. It is concrete-enforced and about the size of a parking space.

They hired jeeps and followed the maps, in order to find it. It wasn't long before they found the well, and as they looked around and noticed a ladder that went down the well. So, each of them went down into went down into the barely lit tunnel of the well, where the maintenance people work, and were looking for a secret passage.

They looked for any kind of clue that may help them. The tunnel they were in was built during the King Solomon's days and leftover were candle holders along the walls, before they installed electricity. So, they pulled down on the candle holders to see if something may happen in their favor.

Once they pulled down the candle holders, to their surprise one of the candle holders was a lever and a cement wall opened slightly to reveal a crevice. It was enough for them to collectively to push aside this ancient brick block and once they did that they found a secret passageway.

As they were navigating through the secret passageway, a scorpion appeared and blocking their path. It was showing aggression by raising his tail over his back. The boys knew to handle this situation with caution, as the girls were sheltering behind them. The boys went into action, because one sting could end one of their lives.

One of the boy's took off his belt and used it like a lasso and whip. He snapped his belt at the scorpion, crushing it and allowing them to pass. They proceeded down the secret passageway until they came to a chamber where could see the pile of gold from a distance. To their alarm, they saw a man in what looked like a British soldier's uniform with only his skeleton remaining. The skeleton held a note.

They looked at the note before proceeding and it said, "I gained access to the chamber in 1900. I made a mistake in my calculations, before I approached the gold. In my haste, I didn't leave the door open to the chamber and the door closed behind me, cutting off my air. So, I'm passing this note along to encourage the next person to keep the door open and don't make the same mistake I made. I'm losing consciousness. Please take my identity tags and let my family members know you found me. Good luck."

The Lawndale Gang took the identity tags and proceeded forward to where the gold was, but they accidentally tripped a detection wire along the ground. Suddenly, the earth opened up creating a separation between the Lawndale Gang members. This separation was a 25-foot valley that was very steep.

However, there were vines hanging from the ceiling, but they were just out of reach. The boys on the other side of the valley took a running leap and jumped on to the vines to swing across to the other safe side. Unfortunately, three of the girls were still on the other side and they had to find a way to transport them safely over the steep valley.

They soon noticed a stream of light that came in through the back of the chamber. The light seemed to connect to the tripwire and they wondered if this stream of light was somehow connected to the whole mechanism that caused the ground open up. So, they got the idea for one of the girls on the other side to go into their pocketbook and get her makeup mirror.

They thought that if the light was capable causing the ground to open up, maybe if they reversed the light back to its source, something might happen in their favor.

The girl took out her makeup mirror and used it to reflect and reverse the light back to its source. They waited and soon felt the ground moving and vibrating under their feet. To their amazement, the ground started to come back together again enough for the girls to walk over to make the gang whole again.

They walked in and saw the legendary gold of King Solomon. They reported to the Israeli government that they found King Solomon's gold. It was found to be worth two billion dollars. They received a 15 percent finder's fee and had a lot to think about regarding what to do with the money.

While taking the long plane ride home and they discussed among themselves what to do with the money. None of them had the opportunity to go off to college and this money could pay for higher education. They didn't regret involvement in their adventures, solving both mysteries and crimes. They came to the collective decision to put their investigative abilities behind them and do something constructive with this money. They were still young enough to go to college and can use the finder's fee to pay tuition and fees for the next four years.

This will be the next chapter in their lives. They learned a lot about themselves along the way and they hoped to teach their children some values they have learned about love, commitment and believing in yourselves. They've been on many adventures, but the most important adventure starts with yourself.

Long live the Lawndale Gang.

Trotter Street

As I moved through life, I married and had three daughters. I moved to Trotter Street with my wife to raise our family. We met five other couples, whom we quickly bonded with, as we attended school, community events and traveled together. We participated in many activities that brought us an abundance of laughter and caring.

A neighbor a few doors down from us was having a birthday party and my wife and I were invited. The wives already knew each other, but the husbands never met. What a surprise it was, when we all truly enjoyed each other's company! The husbands discovered they all had a love for golf, and before the evening was over, we had formed a golfing foursome.

After our golf outing, we sat on the stoop of one of the player's home and had a few beers to reflect on the day. We enjoyed sitting on their stoop and chatting, when someone proposed having a patio party for everyone. Something very special was born that night, which gave us many happy memories in the years to come.

A friendship was born that created a bond that would last a lifetime. We began hosting weekly patio parties, which continued for several years. We would talk and laugh late into the night. We celebrate together and supported one another. We truly cared for one another and felt very connected. We all recognized we had something special amongst ourselves and we were creating lasting memories.

Before long, the Trotter Street Gang began holding block parties. We had six awesome years of block parties. We had pony rides for the kids, dunk tanks, bounce houses, and all kinds of games. We had a fire engine and ladder engine trucks come to our block parties for the children. We would get a two-day permit, so the block was closed for two days so the children could play in the street for an extra day. We even had fireworks to close out the block party! Our block parties were truly spectacular events!

All of our children went to the same parochial school in Philadelphia, played together, and grew up together. Some have continued to be lifelong best friends. We attended each child's Christening, as well as their First Holy Communion.

During the winter, the husbands would watch the Eagles game and take turns hosting the game. In September, one of the members would organize a trip to the Thunderbird Motel in Wildwood, NJ. It was a great deal! $99.00 per person. That included two nights, a meal and an extended happy hour on the second night. We went to the Thunderbird three years in a row. One of our members said, "Most people come to the shore to escape from their neighbors, we come down to the shore to party with our neighbors." We had so much fun! We organized casino bus trips to the casinos in Atlantic City in which many people on the block participated. Those were unforgettable times.

We attended Beef and Beer fundraisers at the Knights of Columbus Banquet Hall several times a year to help raise money. We would dance the night away.

I just turned 65 years old. I am very fond of all the memories I have of Trotter Street. I feel fortunate I could share so many experiences with such a special group of people. We looked out for each other. There was a true sense of caring for one another. It makes me proud that all our children had such a wonderful upbringing on Trotter Street. My three daughters still talk about the wonderful childhood they had, growing up on Trotter Street. We shared a genuine bond, built on joyful memories and shared experiences.

I feel blessed to have had two important groups in my life that greatly impacted me. The center of it all was the endearment of love, which was significant and meaningful for both groups. Let's move forward with love and purpose.

www.ingramcontent.com/pod-product-compliance
Lightning Source LLC
Chambersburg PA
CBHW030344180626
46812CB00007B/2755